VINCENT
and the
GRANDEST HOTEL on EARTH

Also by Lisa Nicol
Dr Boogaloo and the Girl Who Lost Her Laughter

VINCENT

and the
GRANDEST HOTEL on EARTH

Lisa Nicol

PUFFIN BOOKS

PUFFIN BOOKS

UK | USA | Canada | Ireland | Australia
India | New Zealand | South Africa | China

Penguin Random House Australia is part of the Penguin Random House group of
companies whose addresses can be found at global.penguinrandomhouse.com.

First published by Puffin Books, an imprint of
Penguin Random House Australia Pty Ltd, in 2019

Cover design by Rachel Lawston © Penguin Random House Australia Pty Ltd
Cover illustration © Nancy Liang
Typeset by Midland Typesetters, Australia

Printed and bound in Australia by Griffi n Press, part of Ovato, an accredited
ISO AS/NZS 14001 Environmental Management Systems printer

ISBN 978 1 76 089068 1 (Paperback)

 A catalogue record for this
book is available from the
National Library of Australia

Penguin Random House Australia uses papers that are natural and recyclable
products, made from wood grown in sustainable forests. The logging
and manufacture processes are expected to conform to the environmental
regulations of the country of origin.

penguin.com.au

For Kate, Paul, Jacob & Liam

BEFORE WE BEGIN . . .

If I could just take a brief moment to explain something about moments . . .

Not all moments in time are the same. There are *some* moments that change everything. Some moments that set you on a different path, altering your life forever. Some moments, from which no one and nothing will emerge the same.

This story begins with one of those moments.

At first glance such moments can seem incredibly ordinary. It is only looking back, when you're a bag of wrinkles and involuntary farting has become a regular part of your day, that you can see how very MOMENTOUS the particular moment actually was.

MOMENTOUS moments are like that.

They're often long gone before you can see flashing arrows from every other important moment in your life pointing right at them.

Now you, modern reader, have probably already twigged that someone called Vincent has a part to play in this particular moment.

And you'd be right.

But he wasn't alone. So before we begin, let me introduce you to the two people forever tethered to this moment in time. The two people whose worlds were not just shaken but transformed so completely they were as unrecognisable as the life of a butterfly is to a caterpillar. (That gets me to thinking, I wonder if a butterfly remembers being a caterpillar? Safe to say we'll never know, I guess. Life's full of grand mysteries, isn't it?)

Introducing Vincent

Vincent lived in an ordinary town called Barry. The name says it all. The way it falls out of your mouth and sort of drops onto your big toe like a ball of lead.

Barry.

Barry has never, not once, appeared on a bucket

list. Nor a T-shirt like I ♥ New York or London or Paris. In fact the only reason anyone ever came to Barry was to drive *through* it on their way to The Grandest Hotel on Earth. Now Vincent and his family lived on Standard Street, just below Parr Street. His house was ordinary. His clothes were ordinary. And his hair was ordinary too. (Do I need to tell you it was brown?) Average in height, with no unusual or distinguishing features whatsoever – not even a freckle – Vincent was *so* ordinary that being mistaken for someone else was the only time he was noticed at all.

And there was no one of any note in Vincent's family. Made up of fruit pickers and ticket collectors and factory workers, they just got through life as best they could. Much like the rest of us. Of course, no one is truly ordinary once you get to know them and, after THAT MOMENT, Vincent would never be described as ordinary again.

Introducing Florence
Now it's hard to imagine anyone less ordinary than young Florence. She lived at The Grandest Hotel on Earth. Her full name was – as you would expect – extremely grand. It was Florence Vivienne Delilah

3

Everest Wainwright-Cunningham III. Her wardrobe was grand: milk-blue velvet skirts, lace shirts, beaded and feathered hand-stitched jackets. And emerald boots that lit up and played Bach when she walked.

Of course, her family was grand too. Grand in size. Grand in imagination. Grand in talents. Inventors, artists, spies, explorers.

Her Aunt Violet was a famous jazz singer and her Uncle Earl was the first man ever to jump from the edge of space. Already twenty-nine Wainwright-Cunninghams had found their way into the *Guinness World Records* book. And then, of course, there was her parents' hotel! The Grandest Hotel on Earth. *So* grand it *itself* was in *Guinness World Records* as the grandest hotel in all the world – an award anyone with half a chicken's brain could surely have worked out from the name alone. (Did you know the book *Guinness World Records* is in the *Guinness World Records* book? I kid you not. Another one of life's mildly amusing mysteries!)

So let's get cracking, shall we? My co-author just gave me his 'wind it up' signal, which means time to push our story-wagon out onto the street and get moving. Having said that, I'm sure he won't object

4

if I take just one more moment to tell you about him. After all, these days co-authors are as rare as a rap song with no swearing. Which is why I feel so incredibly lucky to have one.

To start with they're useful. Say if I decide to take a little lie-down and it's not yet three o'clock, my co-author whispers in my ear and reminds me that only people who wear nappies nap at this time of day and to get back to my desk. Pronto! He also tells me when my jokes 'suck' – his word not mine. Or when I'm getting muddled up. He's like the big stick (a huggable big stick) and I'm the piñata. Those lollies aren't going to come out by themselves, if you know what I mean. Now there are many authors who don't need a stick (most of them enjoy jogging long distances at dawn, I'm told), but I, modern reader, am not one of them. Honestly, I don't know what I'd do without him. My co-author doesn't just help tell the story; in many ways he *is* the story.

Clear as chunky stew, I know, but once things get underway, you'll understand *exactly* what I mean. Trust me. He'll make sure of it.

Shall we?

CHAPTER 1

THAT MOMENT

And so it was.

In a busy market, on a busy street.

Florence, along with Rupert the hotel's concierge, was looking for a shoeshiner to clean the guests' shoes, since mostly they had no desire whatsoever to clean their own.

Well, that very same morning, Vincent's grandfather died. He had next to no possessions and the only thing he left behind was a shoe-cleaning kit. He had always told Vincent how his shoe-cleaning kit was magic. 'It's taken me around the world and back that kit has. Would never have met your grandmother if it wasn't for that ordinary-looking brush 'n' polish. And then you wouldn't be here, would you, Vincent? You wouldn't have had the chance to enjoy this glorious life you've got now. Explain that! Has to be magic! Has to be!'

Not many people would describe Vincent's life as glorious, but Vincent's family was like that. They delighted in the small things. Because they had to. There *were* no BIG things. No big events or adventures or awards. Well, not until THAT MOMENT anyway.

'Here,' said Vincent's dad, handing him the shoe-cleaning kit. 'Pa would have wanted you to have this. It would make him happy.'

He also gave Vincent a short wooden stool – just the perfect height for cleaning shoes – and the beaten-up old box with a shoe mount on the lid.

Vincent was thrilled! He couldn't remember the last time he'd had such a wonderful surprise. Just out of the blue like that. He couldn't wait to try it out to see if a bit of his grandfather's magic would rub off on him. Not that he wasn't sad about his grandfather dying. He was. But his grandfather had told him many times he was well fed up and at eighty-five he'd had quite enough of life. He said, when you can't pull up your own trousers or enjoy a nice curry and a beer with a bit of pudding because it gives you the runs and you're not nearly as good at getting to the toilet on time as you used to be, it was jolly hard to enjoy life and he was keen to move on.

So Vincent gave his now strangely cold Pa a kiss and a big hug and swiftly took off with his new old shoe-cleaning kit and headed for the market near the train station. All the way, Vincent couldn't stop thinking about what he was going to buy with the money he'd make cleaning shoes. A big fat bag of salt-and-vinegar chips for one thing. And one of those blue sports drinks that looks more like the stuff you squirt in the toilet so you can't see the skid marks in the bowl. And maybe he'd go to the movies! He'd never been to the movies.

When Vincent arrived he decided to set up right next to the train station entrance where the market began. He figured that way he would get the shoppers as well as all the people travelling by train. Straightaway Vincent spotted an empty space next to the snack machine, which happened to have salt-and-vinegar chips and sports drinks! *Is there magic happening already*? wondered Vincent. He sat down on his stool and put the box in front of him. He pulled out a shoe brush and a couple of pots of polish, placing them carefully on top of the box next to the shoe mount. That way, people would know he was a shoeshine boy!

Vincent was SO excited.

He couldn't quite believe he had a job. Not just a job . . . a business! None of the kids at school had one. He thought he must be the only eleven-year-old in Barry with his own business.

Vincent rearranged his brush and polish, making sure it was just right. He tidied his ordinary brown hair with his fingertips and a bit of spit. And as he sat, waiting for his first customer, Vincent began noticing the shoes of every passer-by. *Well, they sure need a polish! I hope they aren't going to work like that! Those high heels are wobbly! I hope she doesn't fall . . . poor lady looks like she's in awful pain. There must be some way to make them more comfortable.*

Immediately, ideas for designing shoes and how to make them better began popping into his head. And at that exact moment, Vincent fell deeply in love with shoes. (Sorry, that moment is not THE moment I was talking about earlier. THAT moment is coming up shortly. My co-author just pointed out I had better clear up that 'mess of moments' or even a gifted and talented reader would surely be confused.)

Before long Vincent's first customer arrived. It was a fat man with a belly so large and perfectly round he looked like he'd swallowed a hopper ball. He probably couldn't see his own shoes let alone clean them.

'How much for a shine, lad?' asked the fat man.

'Ah, um.' Vincent hadn't yet given a thought to how much he should charge. He hesitated. 'How about a dollar?'

'Well, let's see how good a job you do first. If it's good, I'll pay you a dollar. If it's bad, I'll pay you less.'

Vincent agreed. He figured he needed the practice as much as he needed the dollar. The fat man put his shoe on the shoe mount. Vincent rummaged around, found some black polish and got to work. After giving the shoes a thorough shine, he double-checked each one to make sure he hadn't missed a spot.

'There,' he said, 'I think they're done.'

Holding onto the snack machine so he didn't topple over, the fat man heaved up a shoe to inspect Vincent's work.

'Very nice!' he declared, smiling, his third chin disappearing into his fourth, his fourth into his fifth and so on. 'They look brand new!'

A wonderful tingling feeling came over Vincent.

'Here.' The fat man pulled out two dollar coins from his trouser pocket and flicked them at Vincent. They glinted as they spun in the air then dropped onto the pavement. *Ping! Ping!*

Vincent thanked the man and scooped them up. He couldn't quite believe it. He was halfway to a sports drink already!

It didn't take long for Vincent's second customer to arrive and, not long after, another. But an hour or so later, the rush-hour bulge of workers had squeezed its way through the ticket barriers and Vincent's steady stream of customers slowed to a trickle.

As Vincent was tidying up his polishes, along came Florence and Rupert the hotel concierge. (If anyone's wondering what a concierge is, it's the person in a fancy hotel whose job it is to help the guests and fix their problems. Like finding a taxi at 3 am or tracking down 3000 pink rose petals and eighty litres of yak's milk because that's how some posh chump likes to take a bath.)

'What about him?' asked Rupert, pointing at Vincent.

'Well, he has a brush and polish. Nothing grand, but grand is what we do, so that won't be a problem,' said Florence.

'Indeed, indeed, indeed!' agreed Rupert, enthusiastically.

So Florence approached Vincent.

'Excuse me,' she said, 'I'm from the hotel up in the mountains and we're looking for someone to clean our guests' shoes over the summer. It's such a busy time. Would you be interested by any chance?'

Vincent stood up.

'I-I-I . . . would be, y-y-y-yes,' he stuttered as his mind flew up the mountain to the only hotel he knew of there. *Surely not . . . It couldn't be, could it? Could it?*

'What luck finding you so quickly. I thought we'd be here all morning. I'm Florence by the way.'

'Vincent.'

'Pleased to meet you.' Florence offered her hand to shake. But Vincent, in a mild state of shock, just left it hanging there.

'Here's our address,' said Florence, giving him

a business card. 'Can you start tomorrow, by any chance?'

Vincent didn't reply. Instead he read the card four times. Just to be quadruply sure it said what he thought it said.

The Grandest Hotel on Earth
1708 Mountain View Rd
Mount Mandalay
Mabombo Ranges

Apparently it did. There was no other logical conclusion. Vincent decided he was indeed being invited to clean shoes at The Grandest Hotel on Earth!

Florence was used to this sort of reaction. She waited patiently for Vincent to recover and reply. Softly tapping her foot while she waited, her emerald boots played Bach's Cello Suite No.1 in G Major – a tune that sends your heart soaring like a hot air balloon. Around the edges of her boot small lights flashed and twinkled like stars as her toe struck the pavement.

Vincent looked down at her musical emerald boots. 'Bach?'

'Yes!' replied Florence, stunned but now one hundred per cent certain that Vincent was the very right choice to be the shoeshiner at The Grandest Hotel on Earth. 'So . . . is tomorrow too soon?'

Vincent shook his head.

'Wonderful. Everyone who works at the hotel starts off by being our guest. Just for a day and a night. Here's a letter for your parents to explain it all.'

Florence handed Vincent an envelope. 'I hope they let you come. It's the quickest way to get to know how The Grand runs. You can't really understand how we do grand until you experience it for yourself. Guest orientation starts in the lobby. Ten o'clock. They'll be expecting you.'

'Okay,' he squeaked, excitement and disbelief squeezing his voice box till he sounded like a fruit bat.

Vincent could barely believe it.

He wasn't just going to work at The Grandest Hotel on Earth. Tomorrow he was going to be a guest! It felt like surprises were mounting up one upon the other, like scoops of ice-cream. Surely guest for a day had to be the final scoop! The scoop dripping with hot salted-caramel fudge icing, a sprinkling of nuts and a flake sticking out the top. Right now Vincent thought he knew *exactly* how Charlie felt when he found the last golden ticket.

Vincent watched as Florence and the hotel concierge disappeared into the crowded street, at which point he packed up his kit and ran all the way home. A bag of chips and a blue sports drink could hardly compete with The Grandest Hotel on Earth! Was there ever more evidence of the magic his grandfather talked about? Vincent didn't think there could be.

CHAPTER 2

GUEST FOR A DAY

'Wake up, wake up, wake up, wake up!'

Startled, Vincent woke. It was his seven-year-old sister, Rose, shaking him and yelling in his ear.

'I'm awake!' growled Vincent. He rolled over and buried his face in his pillow.

'Get up, Vincent! It's our first day at The Grandest Hotel on Earth. We can't be late!'

Vincent sat up. 'What time is it?'

'It's 5.30 already! And I still need to wash my hair, paint my nails and somehow decide what I'm going to wear.'

'*You're* not coming, Rose,' he said, a mixture of irritated and half asleep.

'MARILYN!' she screeched.

'Marilyn then! But you're still not coming.'

Rose insisted on being called Marilyn. She had big plans to become a movie star and thought Marilyn a far more suitable name than Rose. She also insisted on wearing a blanket everywhere, like a cape, in case she was spotted by one of her fans or the paparazzi. Or 'paps' as Rose called them. Although there were no 'them'!

'But, Vincent, there's bound to be some big-time movie producers staying at the hotel. All I need to do is lurk around and get spotted. It'll be the big break I've been waiting for my *whole* life!' she said, pressing her hands together and squeezing her eyes shut as if she was praying for world peace.

'I'm going to the hotel to work, not lurk. And you're not going there to do either!'

Rose stopped praying. She folded her arms and bit her top lip. She paused dramatically then leant in. 'Why would you want to stand in my way? What have I ever done to you?' She glared at Vincent, as if trying to peer into his soul. 'You're jealous!' she declared, turning in a theatrical swivel, cape flying and stomped out of the room. 'This town's fine for someone ordinary like yourself, Vincent, but *SOME* of us are meant for bigger things.'

Vincent rubbed his eyes. He looked at a postcard of The Grandest Hotel on Earth he'd found on the street, now sticky taped to the wall beside his bed. He'd been awake half the night imagining what the place might be like. He'd heard plenty of stories. The Grandest Hotel on Earth was the kind of place stories swirled around. Bizarre tales of dancing turtles and flying llamas were sworn by some to be true while others dismissed them as absolute nonsense. And the Wainwright-Cunninghams were the kind of people stories swirled around too. And not all the stories were nice. Polite people described the family as 'eccentric', while less-polite people called them crazier than a soup sandwich. But Vincent was determined to put aside all he'd heard and make up his own mind. He leapt out of bed and got dressed. He was so excited he felt sure the needle on his thrill-o-meter must be nudging past Christmas!

Vincent's father was already up and busy. He was at the kitchen sink, filling up a saucepan.

'Morning. If you don't want eggs, you'll have to get your own breakfast. Mum's been up all night with Thom. She's trying to grab twenty winks before I head off.'

Thom was Vincent's little brother. He was four and a half and had not yet spoken a single word. The way things were going Vincent's mum and dad thought Thom would probably need to go to some sort of special school. Although they tried their best not to let on, Vincent could tell it caused his parents a truckload of worry. There were always appointments to go to and tests to be taken. And despite spending every cent they had, so far no one had been able to tell them what exactly was wrong with Thom. He was the reason Vincent had recognised Florence's boots were playing Bach. Classical music was the only thing that calmed Thom down when he was having one of his terrible tantrums, which could go on for hours if he got stuck in a groove. But as soon as he heard Bach or Beethoven or Stravinsky or Shostakovich he immediately stopped screaming and lay on his back – a bit like a starfish – and listened. Unfortunately, he was none too fond of sleeping, so when Thom woke long before dawn, his mum and dad would put on the longest symphony they could find and go back to bed. Gentle swaying piano music coming from the other room was always a telltale sign of a rough night.

'You sure you'll be all right staying overnight at that hotel by yourself?' asked his father, trying to step into his big black rubber workboots and light the stove at the same time. 'I wish I could take up their offer to join you, but you know I can't miss a shift. We're saving every cent we can right now so we can send Thom to see the specialist in town. And there's no way Mum can leave your brother.'

'I'll be fine, Dad,' reassured Vincent, trying to hide his disappointment. 'Who knows, if things go well, maybe there'll be a job there for you too.'

Vincent's dad worked at FishyKittys, a cat-food factory on the outskirts of town. Everyone in Barry worked there. And the smell was the only thing people who came to Barry ever remembered. Most days, from around midday, a disgusting pong drifted into town and sat there till long after dusk. The sort of brown, pongy fog created when 500 kilos of rotting prawns and fish is mishmashed up with a bit of jelly and baked in an oven. Luckily, people in town were used to it. When you breathe in something your whole life, eventually you just don't notice it.

'That'd be nice. Better than shovelling rotten prawns, I bet, but probably as likely as Rose going anywhere without her cape.'

Meaning it just wasn't going to happen.

But if Vincent knew anything, it was that his parents were no good at dreaming. Ever since Thom came along, dreaming had become a luxury item they could no longer afford and getting your hopes up had been reclassified as a dangerous activity.

'I'd better go. I'm late already. Eggs are on.'

Vincent sat down at the kitchen table and watched the sand run through the egg timer. They always had eggs for breakfast. Eggs were the only food Thom ate. Everything else he threw at the wall.

Rose stomped into the kitchen and sat down. She plonked her stripy-socked legs and fluffy plastic slippers, which she loved because they had a bit of a heel, up onto the table. Vincent ignored her. As the very last grain of sand slipped through the hourglass, he got up and lifted the heavy saucepan off the stove. The boiling water swooshed from side to side.

'Ouch!' yelled Vincent, as a wave of hot water rose up the side and splashed onto his hand.

'What did you expect? It's just come off the

stove, you dodo!' said Rose, helpfully. She combed her eyebrows with a toothbrush and tried to look menacing.

'No, really?' said Vincent, sarcastically. He fished an egg out of the pot, knocked the top off and put it down in front of his sister.

'Do you know how many feelings I can do with just my eyebrows?' Rose covered the bottom-half of her face with her cape and moved her eyebrows up and down and all around like two hairy caterpillars having some sort of fit. 'Hundreds!' she declared.

Vincent rolled his eyes.

Rose looked down at the perfectly cooked egg. 'I'm not eating THAT!' she said, shoving it away. 'It's too runny.'

'Suit yourself,' said Vincent. He made his mum a cup of tea and tiptoed down the corridor to his parents' room. Thom was asleep on a mattress on the floor. Vincent still remembered the day his mum and dad came home and let him hold his brand-new baby brother. He was so excited. There was nothing Vincent wanted more than to be a big brother. Of course he already was a big brother to Rose, but Rose didn't seem to want one. She liked to do everything all by herself. And I mean everything.

Her first words were 'Me do it!' and that was how it was. Me do it! So the idea of a little brother he could hang out with and teach stuff to and look after sounded to Vincent like a hit song. Unfortunately, Thom wanted a big brother even less than Rose did. In fact Thom didn't seem to know he even had one. Almost as if Vincent was invisible.

And that was probably the hardest bit of all.

So hard Vincent never gave breath to those words.

Not to anyone. Not even to himself.

Deep down he hoped if he ignored that truth, maybe it would go away.

His mum, still half asleep, put a finger up to her mouth, shushing Vincent to be quiet. She looked tired – more tired than usual – as she stepped over Thom and tiptoed into the hall.

'Don't bring hot drinks into the bedroom,' she whispered sharply, grabbing the cup of tea and heading off to the kitchen. 'You know what your brother's like.'

That was another sure sign of a bad night: cranky parents.

'Feet off the table, Rose,' she said, plonking her tea down.

Rose, still combing her eyebrows with the

toothbrush, did as instructed while trying to lasso Vincent's gaze and drag it over to her egg now teetering half off the other side of the table.

Vincent refused to give her the satisfaction and pretended not to notice.

'Right. Let me take a look at you,' said his mum, pulling her long beautiful hair back into a low bun. She never wore it out these days. In case Thom got a hold of it.

Vincent stood up tall and pulled his shoulders back as she looked him up and down. He tugged at his shirtsleeves that ended just below his elbows. 'They're a bit short.'

'Roll them up. No one will notice,' she suggested.

As Vincent rolled up his sleeves, a crashing sound like something large falling followed by a heavy thud came from the bedroom.

And then another one. *THUD.*

'Oh no. What on earth's he done now? There's nothing left to break in there, I swear!' Vincent's mum hurried back to the bedroom.

'Phone us to let us know you're all right, won't you, Vincent?' she called. 'There should be some money for your bus fare in the bottom of my handbag.'

Vincent dug around till he found enough coins and then dropped them into the plastic bag with his pyjamas. As he did he noticed something was missing.

Vincent lunged across the table.

'ROSE!'

He snatched his toothbrush out of her hand and shoved it back in his bag. Rose mimed a whooping evil laugh and mouthed 'SUCK ON THAT!' at Vincent. For a seven-year-old, Rose had a potty mouth something shocking. Vincent shot her the death stare. Steam rose from his mother's cup of untouched tea, which would almost certainly go cold.

Not quite the send-off he'd hoped for.

Vincent picked up his bag and shoe-cleaning kit and headed out the door.

CHAPTER 3

THE GRANDEST HOTEL ON EARTH

'The Grandest Hotel on Earth!' yelled the bus driver.

Vincent peered out the window. And sure enough, there it was. At the far end of the Mabombo Ranges, perched on the lower slope of Mount Mandalay – The Grandest Hotel on Earth. It looked just like his postcard. Glowing golden yellow in the morning sun, it reminded Vincent of a giant majestic lion watching over its pride.

'You don't go any closer?' he asked, eyes locked on the hotel, which was still quite a fair way off.

''Fraid not,' said the bus driver. 'This is it, boyo.'

Vincent got off the bus. He watched as it turned around and drove back down the winding road towards Barry. He took a deep breath in. The fresh, clean mountain air was a lovely change from the fishy pong of Barry's streets. It made Vincent realise just how stale the air at home had become.

Although it was a little windy, Vincent didn't mind having to walk. As his parents frequently liked to remind him, most things in life rarely turn out to be as good as the time you spend looking forward to them. Even though he thought that was a dreary way of looking at the world, he figured the longer he spent *anticipating* being a guest at The Grandest Hotel on Earth, the better.

Surrounded on all sides by a chain of mountains, Vincent rolled down his too-short sleeves and walked into the wind. He had to put his head down to stop it drying out his eyeballs. As he walked along, Vincent set about daydreaming of the day that lay ahead. *I wonder if we'll get cake for afternoon tea. Or doughnuts! There'll definitely be ice-cream. You couldn't call yourself The Grandest Hotel on Earth if there was no ice-cream! And there's bound to be a pool. I bet it has a diving board! Or a slide! Oh, I hope there's a slide!* While Vincent was having a ball imagining the day ahead, he kept thinking how much *more* wonderful it would be if his dad could have come. Or his mum. *How cool would it be to take them to The Grandest Hotel on Earth!* Vincent tried to remember the last time he'd done anything fun with either of them. Or had one of them all to himself. Apart from doing the shopping. Vincent used to enjoy a trip to the supermarket. It meant a guaranteed packet of bubblegum or a Push Pop or anything else he could slip into the trolley without his mum or dad noticing. But not these days. It was excruciating watching his dad try to add up the cost of all the items in the trolley and count the money in his wallet, or his face at the check-out when he got his sums wrong.

In fact they never went anywhere anymore, even as a family. Which Vincent wasn't entirely sad about. While Thom was bad at home, going out he was a total nightmare. And Barry was a small town. If he did something weird or had one of his epic meltdowns, in no time at all the whole town knew about it. Like the first time they took Thom to the pet store to look at the animals and he started shaking the parrot cage and making weird whooping noises like a gibbon. And neither their mum nor the pet-shop lady could get him to stop. Eventually the parrot just dropped off his perch and lay there, beak down, on the bottom of the cage. Motionless. It must have had a heart attack or something. Vincent had wished he himself was beak down when he saw his classmate Josie run from the pet shop yelling, 'It's dead! He killed it! Vincent's brother just killed a parrot!' He knew by Monday morning everyone in the whole school would have heard all about it and Thom's method of execution would have mutated from shaking the cage into something far more sinister, like biting the parrot's head off.

Most of the way across the plateau, Vincent couldn't see the hotel at all. Either his view was obscured by trees or he was looking at his feet. But after an hour or so of putting one foot in front of the other Vincent looked up. It was like suddenly finding himself on the very edge of the horizon, just as the massive morning sun was rising.

The wind dropped completely.

So did Vincent's jaw and his tongue flopped out like a piece of defrosted steak. He let go of his shoe-cleaning kit, which thwacked onto the ground yet Vincent hadn't heard a sound. As if all his other senses had switched into power-saving mode so his eyes could take in the full magnificence of the vision before him. The hotel was more beautiful, more majestic, more splendid, than Vincent could have ever possibly imagined.

While he knew it was going to be big, he had failed to realise how big until he was up close.

Vincent counted.

It was sixteen storeys high and had what looked like a thousand arched windows and a thousand arched balconies.

And the light!

The air itself was the colour of honey. Some dream-like brew of sunshine and hope. Vincent was so overcome by the blinding beauty of the hotel that he had to prompt himself to do all the things his body usually did without instruction.

Breathe, Vincent.

Blink, Vincent.

Swallow, Vincent.

Put your tongue back inside your mouth, Vincent.

Whatever you do don't pee, Vincent!

Once his brain regained control of his basic bodily functions, Vincent picked up his shoe-cleaning kit and walked through the gates of The Grandest Hotel on Earth.

Surely this must be what the lost paradise of Shangri-la looks like. Or heaven.

In gardens ablaze with colour, everywhere he looked Vincent saw exotic creatures taking in the warmth of the morning sun. White peacocks ambled and twirled across bright green lawns like gigantic snowflakes floating on the breeze. Elephants flapped their ears in unison underneath large trees laden with mangoes. Vincent nearly tripped when a knock-kneed pair of ostriches cut across his path, a bunch of chicks in tow, before disappearing into a grove of trees. He loped after them to catch another glimpse of the birds as big as horses. *Maybe those stories of flying llamas are true!* As he neared the grove his ears filled with the sweetest birdsong. He looked up to see branches full of nightingales and toucans, macaws and kookaburras, and dozens of other foreign feathered fowl perched side by side, preening and singing. Running through the grove was a deep mountain stream so clear Vincent could see fish swimming and otters and platypuses tumbling about. He knelt down. An otter, head out of the water, rolled and swam towards him. 'Aww.

Hello, little fella!' He pushed up his sleeve and tickled its belly. The otter seemed to like it.

'I'm sorry. I'm so sorry,' called out a voice accompanied by low seesawing cello strokes.

Vincent looked up to see Florence, her long cinnamon hair swishing from side to side as she ran briskly towards him. She was wearing the same emerald boots as yesterday at Barry Train Station.

'You made it! I'm sorry, Vincent. I meant to send a car to collect you. We're so out of the way up here.'

'That's okay,' said Vincent. 'It's not every day I get to tickle an otter.'

'True,' said Florence, still puffing. 'But still. No excuse!' She put her hands on her hips as if exasperated with her own incompetence. 'I don't know what's got into me lately. I seem to be forgetting things all over the place. You see most of our guests come by hot air balloon. In fact the last one for this morning should be arriving just about now.' Florence turned and looked over her shoulder and, sure enough, drifting down between two mountains was a huge yellow balloon. 'Much quieter than cars and buses. Traffic noise would destroy the peace and tranquility. And we try not to remind our guests of their day-to-day lives. It's kind of the whole point really. Of course with a hotel of this size we can't rely solely on hot air balloons. There's a tunnel about halfway up the mountain. It runs straight to the basement. For deliveries, that sort of thing.'

Vincent nodded and smiled in an effort to mask the heavy processing going on inside his brain.

'Can I ask a question?' he asked, without realising he already was asking a question.

'Of course,' replied Florence.

'Is that a hippo?' Vincent pointed to a very large creature bounding along the bottom of the stream as if it was wearing spring shoes or walking on the moon.

'It is! Yes!' They watched as the hippo surfaced, took a breath then continued on its lunar way. 'That's Maggie. She's just arrived from Tanzania, but she's already settled in nicely. We've never had a hippo before so we weren't quite sure how she'd go. Now let me help you with your bags.'

Vincent looked down at his plastic bag and beaten-up old box and felt suddenly embarrassed. He wished he had one of those fabulous wheelie suitcases. Even the homeless guy who slept at Barry Train Station had one of those! 'Oh, I-I-I'm good.

I always travel light,' fibbed Vincent, who never travelled at all.

'Me too,' replied Florence. 'There's no need to bring the kitchen sink, is there? I wish some of our other guests were as sensible. There's absolutely nothing you could possibly bring you won't find at The Grand. Trust me.'

Vincent and Florence headed off. As they walked along, Vincent struggled to say anything more intelligent than 'wow' as he listened intently to Florence's running commentary about the exotic animals wandering around and the gardens and the birds. Her knowledge of everything from the laws governing the import of wild animals to the climactic variations of mountainous topographies and how to cross-pollinate roses so they smelt and looked like pink lemonade was positively encyclo-pedic! She explained how The Grandest Hotel on Earth had been built by her great-grandparents after the war, when the world was still in shock and trying to make sense of itself.

'. . . and the Wainwright-Cunninghams have run the place ever since. My parents are away on business so it's just me at the moment.'

Vincent stopped. 'What? Just you?' he said,

trying not to look shocked. 'Are you really in charge of this whole hotel?'

Florence laughed. 'Yes. Just me. And yes, I really am. When you're a Wainwright-Cunningham such things are a fait accompli, I'm afraid.'

Vincent had no idea what a 'fait accompli' meant, but he figured Florence hadn't had a lot of say in the matter.

'Don't get me wrong, it's not that I don't love it,' she explained. 'I mean who wouldn't want to run The Grandest Hotel on Earth?'

Vincent wasn't sure he would, for one! He took a good look at Florence. She was surely about the same age as him and not a day older. 'So where are your parents?'

'You mean today? Bolivia, I believe . . . Oh no, hang on, that was yesterday. That's right, they took the night flight to Turkey.' Florence looked up at the sun. 'It's nine forty-two here, so they'd be landing in Istanbul as we speak.'

'And when are they back?'

'Well, it's three years this June so I can't imagine they'll be *too* much longer. But you never know with these sorts of expeditions. I'm hoping they'll be back sooner rather than later. Especially if this forgetful phase keeps up. I'd hate for something to go wrong while I'm captain of the ship.'

Vincent wondered what sort of expedition could possibly take three years. What were they searching for? Life on Mars? A Himalayan yeti?

'What about you? How long have you been shining shoes?' asked Florence.

'Not *that* long,' replied Vincent, trying to avoid being specific, given he'd been shining shoes for the grand total of one day. 'I inherited my grandfather's shoe-cleaning business fairly recently.' Vincent blinked rapidly as he stretched the truth like a piece of bubblegum. A spot next to the snack machine and a beaten-up old box of polishes could hardly be called a family business.

'How about that!' cried Florence. 'We both run family businesses. I just *knew* when I spotted you at the train station we'd have a lot in common.'

Vincent smiled. But he couldn't imagine why Florence would have arrived at that conclusion. He thought an octopus and box of cereal probably had more in common than the two of them.

'Here we are,' said Florence.

Vincent stopped in his tracks. He felt like he was in a dream, but awake at the same time. Out front was a beautiful lake, a blurry upside-down reflection of the hotel floating across the surface like a field of yellow sunflowers. In the shallows, a flock of pink flamingos, their heads held high, moved as one across the aquatic meadow. As they flicked their black beaks from side to side, Vincent thought they looked as if they were dancing a bird version of the flamenco. He was familiar with the dance because Rose did it everywhere. She stuck drawing pins in the soles of her shoes and stomped about the kitchen, cape flying, snapping her fingers high in the air like they were castanets. Rose insisted every movie star must know how to flamenco. 'If you don't know how to flamenco, you don't know anything about love and if there's one thing a movie star needs to know about, it's love!'

'Come and meet Rupert,' cried Florence as she leapt, two at a time, up the front steps. Vincent, plastic bag swinging, leapt after her. As they reached the top of the stairs, two men in bright blue suits opened the doors:

'Welcome,' they announced, 'to The Grandest Hotel on Earth!'

CHAPTER 4

BINOCULARS AND POCKET DOGS

Vincent dropped his bags again. His lungs stopped inflating and his eyeballs shook.

Vast and soaring, the lobby was the most magnificently beautiful room he had ever stepped foot in. A treasure chest of man and Mother Nature's finest. Emerald-green velvet couches clustered beneath archways hanging with vines that fell like rain. Draped windows three storeys high looking out onto snow-capped peaks. Dogs asleep in front of roaring log fires. Chandeliers made from a thousand moose antlers and coloured glass lanterns that shimmered and dazzled like galaxies. Around the room, tiny ponies – no bigger than medium-sized dogs – with spectacular turquoise feathered headdresses and rainbow tails wandered about with trays on their backs delivering nibbles and drinks. In the centre, beside a clutch of palm trees and double-bass players, a fountain – filled with baby turtles – danced in time to the music. (The fountain that is, *not* the baby turtles. As far as I know turtles don't dance. Although as my co-author just pointed out, only a fool would underestimate a turtle. They did, as he's just reminded me, see off the dinosaurs and can find their way home across vast oceans. Seems unwise, if not arrogant, to suggest they couldn't master a simple waltz or moonwalk.)

Vincent's head rolled back and around as he watched tiny finches streak and flit across a domed gold and midnight-blue ceiling.

Suddenly he felt woozy. He started to wobble.

'Breathe, Vincent,' instructed Florence, before slapping him firmly in the middle of his back.

Vincent took a huge gulp of air. 'Sorry, that keeps happening.'

'Not at all. We're used to a lot of fainting around here. That's why we make sure all our staff at The Grand are well trained in resuscitation. You'll get used to the place. Here comes Rupert.'

Vincent immediately recognised the man trotting towards them as the concierge from the market. He had a brilliantly shiny bald head and a techni-coloured moustache shaped like a smile. He also had a particular way of walking, as if his feet were a little too enthusiastic and further in front than they should to be. His hips, just as enthusiastic, added a wiggly, fallen-on-its-side-figure-eight flourish to each and every step.

'Ah, Vincent! Welcome, welcome, welcome!'

Vincent went to shake hands, but instead Rupert pulled him into a bear hug. 'Oh, no no no, we're huggers here at The Grand, boy!' Vincent strained to manoeuvre his head out of Rupert's armpit as politely as he could so he could suck in a lungful of air. His need for oxygen was starting to resemble a fish that'd jumped out of the water and accidently landed on a rock. And in fact, that was sort of how Vincent felt – like he'd suddenly landed in another almost unrecognisable world.

'I'll see you later, Vincent,' said Florence, dis-appearing behind the front desk. 'I'd join you, but I have a four-truck delivery of Swiss chocolate about to arrive. If they're not unloaded before noon, there won't be enough chocolate for the breakfast fountains tomorrow. Peppy will take your bags.'

Rupert released Vincent as Peppy – one of the dog-sized ponies – arrived to collect his bags.

'Guest orientation's just about to start. Come with me,' said Rupert.

Marble fountains spurting melted chocolate splashed across Vincent's mind as he followed Rupert's wiggly hips over to a group of guests gathered near the palm trees. Everyone was staring up at the ceiling.

'Looks like we have a live one,' said Rupert.

Vincent looked up and saw what everyone was staring at. It was a young boy dangling from a moose-antler chandelier. *Crikey! What's he doing?*

'Get down, Max!' cried the boy's mother. 'You're making a spectacle of yourself! Have you forgotten what happened last time you swung from a light fitting?'

'Your mother's rrr-right, Max,' agreed Rupert. 'Although I do think you'd look *marvellous* with a pair of moose antlers, there's over a hundred kilos of antler up there. Somehow I don't think you could quite carry that off.'

Max's mother climbed up onto an armchair and tried to grab her son by the ankle.

'Nuh-uh,' cried Max, pulling up his legs and sending the chandelier into a swing. This seemed to please Max, who began thrusting his body forwards and backwards to get it swinging even more. 'Woo hoo!'

The chandelier let out a strange groan almost like a real moose.

The crowd of guests gasped and scattered.

'Max, I beg you! Please! GET DOWN!' cried his mother, the corners of her mouth flapping with fear and some kind of permanent crumbling exhaustion.

'Vincent, why don't you have a go?' said Rupert.

'What?'

'Don't panic. You'll think of something. Everyone else, follow me. Welcome drinks are on the balcony. You must all be *dying* of thirst! Come, come, come,' he gobbled, not unlike a turkey.

Everyone except Vincent and Max's mother shuffled off at speed.

Vincent stood there in a state of shock. What on earth was he supposed to do? How on earth was he going to get mad Max down from the chandelier?

Meanwhile Max's mother kept begging and flapping while Max kept right on swinging.

Fear filled Vincent's stomach and climbed up his throat.

Then he had an idea.

Magic tricks! Vincent had taught himself a bunch of them – one of many failed attempts to get Thom's attention. Anything was worth a try.

'Hey, Max,' he said. 'Look at this.' Vincent lifted up his arms and arranged his fingers so it looked as if he was pulling off the end of his thumb and putting it back on again. Max squinted to see what Vincent's fingers were doing. Then he let go of the chandelier and fell into the armchair like a tangle of freshly cooked spaghetti into a bowl. He scrambled out and dashed over to examine Vincent's detachable thumb.

'Oh, thank you, thank you, thank you!' cried Max's mother.

Vincent's shoulders, which had been up around his ears, dropped back down into their usual position. He let out a sigh of relief and they headed off to catch up with the others.

'Well done, Vincent,' said Rupert, as the three of them arrived on the balcony. 'My moustache told me you'd have that sorted out quick smart.

Don't like to boast, but I do have the most sensitive moustache this side of Kathmandu!'

Vincent gave Rupert a hesitant 'no problem' wave and hung at the back of the group. He couldn't believe Rupert had appointed him with the task of rescuing Max! Did he usually outsource disaster management to eleven-year-old new arrivals? What if Max had fallen? Or the chandelier? And what on earth is a sensitive moustache?

'Now gather rrr-round, gather rrr-round, gather rrr-round, everyone, and *welcome* to The *Grandest* Hotel on Earth!' announced Rupert.

The view from the balcony was magnificent. You could see from one side of the valley right across to the other. Vincent began to recover and took a first real look at his fellow guests. He was surprised by what a mixed bunch they were. He had assumed everyone at The Grandest Hotel on Earth would be super posh, and some were, but others looked like they'd just knocked off work from FishyKittys. Their clothes were old. Their eyes tired. Their shoes scuffed.

'My name's Rrr-rupert,' he continued with a drum-rolling 'R'. 'I'm the concierge here at The Grand. If you need anything, I'm your man. Don't be shy. There's not a rrr-request or problem I haven't heard before. Rrr-right. First things first. Transport. As you can see, the hotel grounds are rrr-rather vast. At the bottom of the stairs here we have Guest Transport,' Rupert signalled with both his hands not unlike the way cabin crew do on an aircraft when pointing out the exits in a safety demonstration. 'Here you can collect a jet pack or llama, whichever you'd prefer.'

Jet pack or llama! Are you kidding me? Vincent had no doubt what he'd be choosing and it didn't rhyme with chicken parmigiana.

'Of course you're more than welcome to walk,' added Rupert. 'We have old-fashioned maps for rrr-ramblers. Ah, wonderful!' Rupert clapped his hands together. 'Here come welcome drinks, binoculars and pocket dogs.'

Pocket dogs! Vincent's heart skipped a beat. *Pocket dogs!* He spun round to see a line of hotel staff wheeling trollies towards them. One trolley was full of smoking, multicoloured drinks decorated with slices of fruit and cocktail umbrellas. Another trolley had rows and rows of black binoculars stacked high like some modern art sculpture. And the last trolley had a woven basket full of tiny, *tiny* dogs, their front paws and noses just poking over the edge.

Vincent had *always* wanted a dog. He'd asked for one every birthday and Christmas since he could say 'woof woof'. But Barry was a cat town. That was because everyone who worked at FishyKittys was entitled to half-price cat food. Unfortunately for Vincent though Thom enjoyed squeezing cats, which at no time had turned out well – for Thom or the cat. So Vincent had never actually had a pet of any description. Unless you include the time he built an ant farm in a jam jar. But it's hard to love an ant.

'Pocket dogs stay with you for the duration of your time at The Grand and, yes, *of course* they're allowed to sleep in your bed!' Rupert swivelled towards the middle trolley. 'Binoculars, now these are not your garden variety. And at this altitude the sky's clear enough to see the golf balls those messy Apollo astronauts left on the moon.'

'Ooh, I want to see,' cried Max. He snatched a pair of binoculars off the trolley. Regrettably he picked a pair from the bottom of the pile, not the top, sending the entire sculpture tumbling to the floor.

'Oh my gawd!' groaned Max's mother. She grabbed another smoking drink, tipped it down her throat and began eating the small umbrella on the side.

Vincent felt bad for her. He knew exactly what it was like to be with the badly behaved kid. People looked at you as if it was somehow your fault.

'Never mind, never mind, never mind,' said Rupert, who had a habit of saying things in threes. Half a dozen staff appeared out of nowhere and began gathering up the binoculars and stacking them back on the trolley. Rupert smiled at Max's mother. He took her hand and gave it an understanding squeeze.

'Over this way, boys,' said the parents of three large youngsters with noses that would have made excellent ski jumps at any Winter Olympics. 'Come and choose a rocket dog! They look just like those critters you love blowing up in Battle for Beejaa III.' Mr and Mrs Ski-Jump-for-a-Nose jostled their offspring as far away from Max and his crumbling mother as they could.

With eyes glued to their phones, the boys had not yet noticed a single thing going on around them. Not Max swinging from the chandelier, not the spilt binoculars and not the trolley full of pocket dogs. The three boys grunted and whined that they were right in the middle of a game.

'We'll pass on the rocket dogs,' announced Mrs Ski-Jump-for-a-Nose. 'Our boys are not really fond of animals. In fact they're not very fond of living things.'

'If we're not having snocket dogs, I'll be expecting some sort of discount,' announced Mr Ski-Jump-for-a-Nose to no one in particular.

(Rupert was used to extremely wealthy guests asking for discounts. They were often very attached to their money.)

'Aw they're SO CUTE!' squealed a lanky girl with blue hair – not unlike the colour of Vincent's favourite sports drink. 'I want two.'

'There's just one dog each, Chelsea dear,' explained her father.

'Well, I'm having two because I'm *such* a big animal lover.'

'All right, dear,' replied her father, his droopy eyes and droopy arms drooping a fraction more. 'You have mine. I'll go without.'

'Yay!' Chelsea began fishing about in the basket, examining and tossing dogs aside as if she was selecting a piece of fruit.

Hovering to one side of the basket and clutching his hands together, Vincent waited excitedly while the other guests made their selection. His eyes were locked on a shaggy black-and-white pup sitting smack bang in the middle of the basket. It was no bigger than a teacup and the cutest dog he had *ever* seen.

When it was finally Vincent's turn, he was almost trembling. A tingling feeling spread out from his feet and trickled down into each toe.

Only one dog remained.

It was the shaggy black-and-white pup he'd had his eye on.

He reached in and looked at her name tag: Jess.

'Jess. Hello, Jess,' he whispered. The puppy looked up at Vincent with big smiling eyes. The entire world around them blurred into a colourful smudge. Sound evaporated and time was swept away by the wind. Vincent scooped Jess up, but just as he was lifting her out of the basket a hand smashed through the colourful smudge, swooped down and snatched Jess right out of his hand.

'Awww, this one's even cuter!' squealed Chelsea. She tossed her first choice of pup back into the basket and, with a dog in each hand, sashayed off to show her father.

Vincent was flabbergasted! He looked down at the poor fluffy ginger pup she'd just discarded. He gently picked it up and gave it a cuddle. He could feel its tiny heart thumping. Vincent flipped over her name tag: Min.

'You're okay, Min,' he said, holding her to his chest and stroking her. 'My name's Vincent.' Min looked right at him with her big brown eyes and furrowed brow. Her tiny tail wagged like crazy against his hand.

If Vincent's time at The Grandest Hotel on Earth had ended then and there, he still would have been the happiest boy in the world.

'Rrr-righto, if everyone's selected their pocket dogs, we'll head off to Guest Transport, shall we? This way.' Rupert trotted down the front steps of the hotel.

Vincent popped Min in his top pocket, slurped on a drink till his straw made rude sounds and, humming with excitement, headed off with the group.

CHAPTER 5

THE GRAND TOUR AND ABANDONED DREAMS

'That's it, everyone. Come on in, there's plenty of rrr-room. Now because there's a lot of ground to cover on a grand tour we like to use jet packs.' Rupert gestured to a wall lined with racks of space-age-looking, rocket-shaped backpacks. He used his cabin-crew double-hand signal again as if pointing out the overhead lockers. Rupert seemed to enjoy hand signals immensely. 'Luckily rrr-riding a llama comes quite naturally to most of our guests,' said Rupert. He flicked both his hands across to the other side of the room where a line of shaggy llamas sat chewing on clumps of grass. The long-necked creatures stared at the guests, who were now staring back at them. 'But jet packs can be tricky,' continued Rupert, flicking both hands back again, which really did seem like overkill as it was hard to imagine any guests might *still* be confused as to which was a jet pack and which was a llama.

'Without a bit of jet-pack practice we end up with guests dropping out of the sky like Santa Claus in a cyclone.'

A member of the transport staff began fitting out Vincent with his jet pack. He had to keep reminding himself what was really happening. *I am about to fly! I am actually about to fly!* He placed his forearms along the armrests, which jutted out the front, and wrapped his hands around the control sticks. The jet pack was so light! Not much heavier than his schoolbag.

'Don't push any buttons or move the control sticks till we're outside,' instructed Rupert and almost on cue Max shot up to the ceiling and stuck there, like a dragonfly trying to escape through a skylight.

'Aaargh!' cried Max, who was for some reason now pedalling as if he was riding a bike.

'Oh, quick! Somebody help him!' cried his

mother, who immediately started moving the control sticks in both her hands every which way, sending herself flying about the room like a rapidly deflating balloon.

Vincent and the guests ducked.

The llamas looked up.

'Excuse me,' said an annoyed-looking business-man, clutching his phone over his head, 'how long's all this going to take? I've got calls to make.'

'Don't worry,' said Rupert, crouching on the floor with his hands over his bald head, 'you'll have time for that later, Mr Cash. Now, Max, move the stick in your left hand towards you. *Slowly*.'

Max dropped straight down onto the floor like a drone with a flat battery. Luckily, the floor was soft. Probably for this type of incident. There's always one. More often two.

'Slowly,' repeated Rupert, turning to the boy's mother, who was now stuck up in the far corner of the room, facing the wall.

'Left hand towards you, madam. Gently now!'

Slowly, Max's mother sort of slid down the wall like a blob of something runny. (I was hoping to leave what *sort* of blob up to your imagination, but my co-author is in my ear saying that I should just call a 'blob of snot' a 'blob of snot' and be done with it. He's probably right.) Vincent offered Max's mother a hand up. The poor woman looked like she wanted to curl up and go to sleep and never wake up.

'Rrr-right we are then,' said Rupert. 'Let's get out into the open and have a go, shall we?'

Once outside, the guests placed their pocket dogs on the lawn and started practising. Vincent noticed a young girl with a patch over one eye and a very wobbly walk. She looked particularly delighted as she flew around free of her wobbles.

'Just rrr-remember, left hand up and down, rrr-right hand all around and you should be fine,' instructed Rupert through a megaphone, which he seemed to be enjoying almost as much as his hand signals.

For someone who'd never even ridden a bike, Vincent got the hang of it remarkably quickly. Before long he'd mastered take-offs and landings and was flying around in circles a few metres above the ground. The feeling was unbelievable. *I'm flying! I really am flying!*

Vincent tried to help the ski-jump-for-a-nose boys as they shot up and down like plump frogs attached to backyard fireworks.

'Waaagh!' *Clunk*.

'Waaagh!' *Clunk*. *Thump*.

'Waaagh!' *Clunk*. *Thump*. *Clunk*.

But they ignored Vincent and instead became extremely annoyed.

'These jet packs suck,' complained one of the boys. 'They don't work properly!'

'Yeah!' said another. 'And we'd know. We've flown jet packs millions of times on Battle for Beejaa III.'

'In which case I think a discount is in order,' insisted their father.

Rupert explained that flying a jet pack in a game was quite different to real life.

'You're just too FAT!' yelled Max. 'Fat fat fat fat fat fat fat!'

'Oh! I'm sorry, I'm so sorry so,' babbled Max's mother, incoherent with embarrassment.

'You should be!' screeched Mrs Ski-Jump-for-a-Nose. 'My boys may be a little on the chubby side, but your son is a fully fledged lunatic.'

While the hotel was otherworldly, Vincent felt like the guests were all too familiar.

Once the squabbling died down and everyone was able to use their jet packs reasonably well, The Grand tour got underway. With Rupert in the lead the guests took off and fell into a V formation just like a flock of geese. Once they'd reached the far side of the lake Rupert signalled for everyone to land.

'Marvellous! Just a few wet feet.' Rupert twiddled his blown-about moustache back into position. 'Now this beautiful island in the middle of the lake is called Fin's Island. And it's quite unique! Due to a freakish yet most fortunate coming together of rrr-rare climactic irregularities, it has developed its own microclimate. Despite being almost 3500 metres above sea level, it's a very small tropical rrr-rainforest. Completely unheard of at this altitude. We've had all sorts of botanists and biologists and climate scientists here and none of them can explain it. Which is exactly how we like it at The Grand. There's nothing grander than a mystery. Who wants everything to be explainable, I ask you?'

'I do. I hate mysteries,' declared Mrs Ski-Jump-for-a-Nose. 'I prefer to know absolutely everything.'

'Quite. Now the island is home to over fifty orangutans,' continued Rupert, 'and a large colony of sloths.'

'Sloths! OMG, I love sloths. Daddy, can I swap my pocket dogs for a sloth, can I?' Chelsea pulled the two dogs out of her pocket and roughly shoved them into her father's chest.

'The sloths stay on the island, I'm afraid,' explained Rupert. 'They're complete homebodies and not the least bit fond of travelling.'

Chelsea snatched back her pocket dogs and pulled a face.

'I sympathise with you, Chelsea. We're all *big* sloth lovers here at The Grand,' said Rupert. 'Make sure you get along to one of our "Find Your Inner Sloth" classes rrr-run by our sloth-keeper, Fin. They start most days around three. You can pedal across or canoe.' Rupert pointed to a gaggle of white swan pedal boats and Indian-style canoes.

'Rrr-righto, everyone. Let's move on. We've got lots of ground to cover.' Rupert and the guests took off again. As they flew along, Rupert pointed out some of the 350 species of bird and 1300 animals that called The Grand home. The variety of inhabitants was far more weird and wonderful than any African game park. There were giraffes, kangaroos, gazelles, camels, bears and now hippos. Rupert explained how all the animals had come from illegal zoos or been snatched from the clutches of poachers. Apparently Florence's Aunt Jane, a famous animal-rights warrior, had single-handedly rescued each and every one. 'The climate here means she can bring in animals from almost anywhere on Earth.'

'She can't be *that* famous,' interrupted Chelsea still sulking about the sloths, 'I've never heard of her!'

'Well, Aunt Jane is not one to blow her own trumpet, Chelsea. In her line of work it doesn't pay to be rrr-recognised. When you're trying to outrun a pack of rrr-rhino poachers with AK-47s, it helps if you can blend in with the crowd.'

'Why's that man vacuuming the grass?' asked Max, pointing to a person below. Vincent looked down. There was a man and he did appear to be vacuuming the grass.

'He's not vacuuming,' explained Rupert. 'He's one of our pooper-scoopers.'

'Pooper-scoopers?'

'Yes. Pooper-scoopers. You'll see them all over the hotel because there's just nothing grand about stepping in poop! Particularly elephant poop!'

Vincent switched his jet pack onto autopilot and looked down through his binoculars. While he would have taken any job he'd been offered at The Grand, he felt a mild flush of relief that he was going to be shining shoes and not scooping up elephant poop.

'Elephant poo! Hahahahah! Elephant poo! Can I have a go?' laughed Max. 'I'd like to suck up a big sloppy elephant poo and then slam it into reverse and shoot it into the sky! What a poo storm that would cause! Hahahahaha! Get it? POO STORM . . . Hahahaha!' Max made a noise that sounded like a cross between a plop and a machine gun. *PLOO PLOO PLOO PLOO PLOO PLOO!*

'MAX!' screeched his mother.

'Elephant poo's not sloppy, Max, it's quite firm. Now did I mention the birdwatching here at The Grand? It's *Ab*solutely spec*ta*cular!' said Rupert, obviously eager to steer the conversation away from poo. 'Hence the binoculars! See that meadow of wildflowers?' Double hand signal to the right. 'That's Hummingbird Heath. If you look closely, you'll see it's absolutely thick with hummingbirds. In summer the humming's so loud it sounds like a motorcycle grand prix.'

On they flew over orchards filled with exotic fruits, a huge skate park and go-kart track, an ice rink, roller rink and every sort of court and field you could imagine. A huge outdoor chessboard with pieces the size of well-fed toddlers. A series of swimming pools with waves, waterfalls and slides tossing children into the air like pizza dough. A fun park, hot springs, giant swings, trampolines and trapezes and the surrounding mountains themselves full of hiking tracks, boulders to climb and slopes to ski. There was even a platform halfway up for hang-gliding, parachuting and any other reckless activities that involved hurling yourself off the side of a mountain.

After a banquet lunch at Tenzing – the rotating glass restaurant at the top of Mount Mandalay – and afternoon tea with dozy snow monkeys at the hot springs, Rupert thought it was almost time to get everyone settled in their rooms. 'Rrr-righto,' he said, 'we've time for one last stop.'

What else could there possibly be? wondered Vincent.

Vincent and the other guests followed Rupert on foot to a faraway field.

'Here we are,' declared Rupert.

Where's here? thought Vincent, swatting away overgrown grasses that were tickling the backs of his knees like annoying flies. All he could see were rusty old bits of machinery and piles of rubbish.

'What *is* this place?' spat Mrs Ski-Jump-for-a-Nose nervously. 'Why on earth have you brought us here? It's nothing but a dump.'

Vincent found himself agreeing with Mrs Ski-Jump-for-a-Nose. *Why would Rupert bring us to the hotel dump?*

'I've no reception!' whined a ski-jump-for-a-nose boy.

'Me neither,' said another.

As the guests expressed a chorus of dissatisfaction, Vincent walked around. He started noticing that what at first glance had looked like piles of rubbish were in fact small shrines. Pyramids of beautifully balanced stones and deadwood and broken things. Some had flags on top fashioned out of faded bits of clothing. Others a rusted toy robot, an old dog collar, a large button cracked by the sun. Vincent felt a strange sensation, as if something passed through him. He shivered. *Must be a cold breeze coming off the mountain.*

'This is our Junkyard of Broken and Abandoned Dreams,' declared Rupert. 'Here you can find new dreams or lay some of your old ones to rrr-rest.'

Most of the guests looked as if they had just been presented with a detailed explanation of intergalactic black holes. Including Vincent. He couldn't imagine at all how a junkyard of dreams could possibly work. Or why a fancy hotel like The Grand would have one. *How do you get rid of dreams? And why would you want to? Weren't dreams a good thing?* Vincent thought the hours he whiled away dreaming were often the times he enjoyed the most.

And then he felt it again. That strange sensation of something passing through him. Right through him. *Could it be a dream? Could I have walked through someone's discarded dream?* The thought unnerved Vincent. He found it a little creepy and strange and he was keen to move on.

'You call this grand?' screeched Mrs Ski-Jump-for-a-Nose. 'You'd have to have a few kangaroos loose in the top paddock to call this dump grand! I don't care how big the buffet breakfast is. Boys, we're leaving!'

'Not without a full refund,' chipped in Mr Ski-Jump-for-a-Nose.

'I know it doesn't look very grand,' Rupert reassured everyone, 'but that's because we make the mistake of thinking grand is all about size or luxury. When rrr-really grand has nothing to do with either and *everything* to do with soothing the soul.

Which is why we like to say *sometimes everyone deserves a bit of grand*.'

Vincent remembered what Florence had said at the station: *You can't understand how we do grand until you experience it for yourself*. His mind rumbled and churned like a tropical storm cloud.

Rupert fired up his jet pack and ascended a few metres into the air. 'Rrr-right we are then. Let's head back and get you lot settled.'

CHAPTER 6

ROOMS

Back at the front desk, Rupert began allocating rooms for the new guests. 'How we do this is I make suggestions and you pick whatever rrr-room appeals,' he explained.

'First, Mrs Peters. I think you and Max might enjoy our Inflatable Rrr-room.' Rupert always recommended the Inflatable Room to families with children who couldn't be left alone for a second without wreaking havoc and raining down disaster upon everyone. Then their parents could take a load off and have a small drink in the lounge, knowing their darling little hellraisers were safe and sound and not getting up to any mischief that might break the bank of China. 'Every piece of furniture is inflatable. Max, you can bounce off the walls as much as you like in there. Alternatively there's the Fluffy Rrr-room where everything's fluffy. Or the Pouch Rrr-room. Both wonderfully calming.'

'THE INFLATABLE ROOM! THE INFLAT-ABLE ROOM!' yelled Max.

A completely frazzled Mrs Peters looked relieved and decided the Inflatable Room would be perfect. Rupert winked at her and leant across the front desk. 'Did I mention it is *completely* fireproof too?' he whispered. 'He could throw a Molotov cocktail in there and nothing would so much as smoulder.'

Mrs Peters exhaled and did her best to arrange her exhausted face into a smile. It had been so long her facial muscles struggled to recall what to do.

A porter scooped Max up onto his shoulders, grabbed their bags and off they went. Max could be heard yelling 'Giddy up!' and 'Faster faster!' until they disappeared out of sight.

Next up were an old man and his grand-daughter. Vincent couldn't help but notice they had the saddest eyes.

'Ah, Grandpa Peach and lovely Lily. Oh, how we *love* grandparents at The Grand! I guess that's stating the obvious. Now how about the Levitation Rrr-room? Incredibly uplifting! Or the Laughter Rrr-room? As long as you're not wearing tight clothing or you'll burst your buttons. Oh no,' said Rupert, consulting the bookings book again. 'You're here for a week. More than a night in the Laughter Rrr-room is exhausting. What about our Sparkles Rrr-room? You've never seen anything quite as sparkly. And the bathroom's full of lovely sparkly things – sparkly lip gloss, sparkly shampoo, even the bathwater twinkles. It's phosphorescence, all natural. Just switch off the lights before you jump in. And there's sparkly bathrobes too of course.'

The sparkly bathrobes clinched it and Grandpa Peach and Lily practically twinkled themselves as they headed off to their room.

Next up was the little girl with the wobbly walk and her mother, who clutched her hand tight as a bird's claws on a branch in high winds.

'Ah, April! I have *just* the rrr-room for you,' said Rupert. 'It's the Baby Memories Rrr-room, where you can rrr-remember absolutely everything since the minute you were born. Your first cuddle, your first warm bath, the first time you heard a bird! *Wondrous!*'

Vincent thought remembering meeting his mum and dad for the first time would be incredible! *I wonder what I was thinking?*

Rupert bent down and whispered in April's ear 'It's one of our *most* special rrr-rooms only available for our *most* special guests.'

April smiled and looked up at her mum, who nodded.

'Oh look, here comes Polly,' said Rupert. 'She'll take you to your rrr-room.' A tiny pony trotted over. She had on a large headdress – a dramatic pinwheel of red and turquoise beads and magnificent eagle feathers. April wrapped her arms around the pony's neck. An attendant appeared, lifted her up onto Polly's back and off they trotted to the Baby Memories Room.

Next up was the D'Silva family (previously known as the Ski-Jump-for-a-Nose family, which – I'll admit – was a tad rude and disrespectful but, as my co-author pointed out, frighteningly accurate.) None of the D'Silvas had been the least bit impressed with The Grand. The boys barely looked up from their phones while Mr and Mrs D'Silva seemed to find a problem with pretty much everything. Apparently they'd stayed in every single one of the

world's most expensive hotels – a piece of informa-
tion they were extremely skilled at dropping into
every conversation. You could have asked them for
the time and their answer still would have begun
with: 'Well, when we were staying at The Royal
Palace in Morocco . . . Blah blah blah.' You get the
idea, right?

'What about the Rrr-room of the Unexpected?'
suggested Rupert, gleefully. 'Many of our well-
travelled guests enjoy the unexpected.'

'Definitely not. We hate surprises. The D'Silvas
are natural-born leaders,' said Mrs D' Silva. 'We
like to be in control at *all* times.'

'And plus, you never know what a surprise is
going to cost!' chimed in Mr D'Silva.

'Well, how about a bit of indoor skiing? Our
Winter Wonderland Rrr-room has *brilliant* powder
at the moment.' Rupert made skiing motions,
poking his bottom out and shifting his weight from
side to side as if he was flying down a slalom course
at high speed.

'No,' snapped Mrs D'Silva, shaking her head
vigorously. 'We only ever ski Aspen. And the last time
we went the boys refused to leave the lodge. There
was no wi-fi on the slopes. Can you believe that?'

'Rrr-right you are,' replied Rupert, happily. He was used to fussy guests. 'The African Sky Rrr-room? You'd swear you were on the plains of Africa and the feeling of space is truly transcendent.'

'Most certainly not. The African plains are for dung beetles *not* the D'Silvas,' declared Mrs D'Silva.

'What about our Tropical Island Rrr-room? It's Caribbean to be precise.' Rupert's hips appeared to be hearing a band of steel drums from Trinidad and Tobago as they wiggled about while the top half of his body remained mysteriously still.

Mrs D'Silva rolled her eyes. Her lips squirmed like poisoned slugs. 'We've just come from Barbados. Weren't even allowed to drive our 4WD onto the beach! Something about nesting turtles. I mean, I ask you, how were we supposed to get to the water . . . *walk*?'

'Indeed,' said Rupert. 'Hmmm. What about our Butterfly Rrr-room? There's over ten thousand different species. It's enchanting. Like being inside a kaleidoscope. And you wouldn't expect it but they're terribly affectionate butterflies.'

'No. Definitely not. Flappy things. Dis*gust*ing. And where there are butterflies there's bound to be caterpillars. Re*volt*ing.'

'Hmm, that's the Glow-worm Rrr-room out then. The Baby Owls and Toy Train Rrr-room perhaps? The train track goes rrr-right rrr-round the rrr-room perimeter and these baby owls just seem to *love* it! They rrr-ride around for hours. It rrr-really is one of my *favourite* rrr-rooms. Wait till you see them hop on and off, all fluff and eyes and tiny beaks,' enthused Rupert, totally unable to hide his passion.

'No animals! Unless we're selecting them for dinner! Hahaha,' laughed Mrs D'Silva. When she laughed she threw her head back and you could see right up her nose.

'Of course.'

'Crashing Waves Rrr-room?'

'If we wanted waves, we would have gone on a cruise, man.'

'The Sunrise Rrr-room? The view is spectacular!'

'Gawd, no. We like to lie in.'

'How about the Sunset Rrr-room then? The whole rrr-room is bathed in the most beautiful golden light. It truly is otherworldly.'

'What if it's cloudy?' piped up Mr D'Silva. 'We'll take it if you give us a written guarantee there'll be no clouds. And a full refund if there is!'

'The Virtuoso Rrr-room? You can pick up any instrument and play it like an absolute master.'

'The D'Silvas don't play, Rupert. People play for the D'Silvas.' Mrs D'Silva pursed her lips tight like a cat's bottom.

'The Breathtaking Rrr-room?'

'Don't tell me. It's breathtaking?' replied Mrs D'Silva, sarcastically. 'I'm *so* bored with breathtaking.'

'Anti-gravity Rrr-room?'

The three boys looked up from their phones, blinked, then returned to their screens.

'Do we look like astronauts to you?' snapped Mrs D'Silva.

'Milky Way Rrr-room? It's on the top floor. Brilliant stargazing. It's not unusual to see hundreds of falling stars in a single night. In fact the lass who's in the *Guinness World Rrr-records* for seeing the most falling stars *did* so in our Milky Way Rrr-room!' declared Rupert, proudly, his head wobbling like a dashboard doggy.

'Falling stars are so overrated. I have no idea why people get excited by a bit of burning rock. Do you, Harold?'

'No, dear, I don't.'

Vincent was shocked. He would have given anything to see a falling star, but the brown pongy fog from FishyKittys ruled out any sort of stargazing in Barry. The D'Silvas turned their already turned-up noses at everything! Vincent thought it a mystery how Rupert didn't bonk them on the head.

Everyone except Rupert was surprised when the D'Silvas settled on *La Chambre de Pommes Frites*, which is just a standard hotel room except for two small sliding doors in the wall. Every time you open the first door you're presented with a bowl of freshly cooked hot chips, a side order of chicken salt and tomato sauce. No matter how fast you open it! (Or how many times. Those D'Silva boys gave it an absolute flogging.) The second door took away the empty bowls, so no one could ever know how many you'd actually eaten. Not even the cleaners. Rupert had found a lot of posh people liked *La Chambre de Pommes Frites*, which was French for the Hot Chips Room.

'Ah, Mr Cash,' said Rupert, looking at the stressed-out businessman who was now twitching in time to the constant stream of message alert dings on his phone. 'I highly rrr-recommend the Rrr-room of the Short Pause. You just have to rrr-remember, when you turn on a tap, it'll be a minute or two before the water flows. Same with the lights. Even if you open the window expect a short pause before the breeze arrives. Trust me, you'll be rrr-relaxed in no time. Or perhaps the Transit Rrr-room? It's just like a bustling airport lounge. Here at The Grand we find terribly busy people like yourself struggle to rrr-relax unless you're on your way somewhere.'

A look of hope flashed across the tired business-man's face. 'You're right! I'm always missing my plane because I've fallen asleep in the gold-class lounge. And the rest of the time I can't sleep. I'll take it,' Mr Cash picked up his briefcase and dashed off, twitching, to the Transit Room.

Next up was Chelsea. She turned down the Bird's Nest Room, the Jelly Pool Room, the Cloud Room, the Moonlit Room and the Rocking-Horse Racetrack Room before settling on the Arcade and Roller-coaster Room. Her poor father looked queasy and turned the colour of an uncooked prawn when he discovered even the beds were attached to roller-coasters.

'Don't worry,' whispered Rupert into Chelsea's dad's ear. 'The Arcade and Rrr-roller-coaster Rrr-room adjoins the Japanese Wishing Well

Rrr-room. You can slip on a kimono and slide in there when you've had enough of the Midnight Dipper and make a wish or two. *Extremely* tranquil.'

Chelsea's father looked relieved and scurried off after his daughter.

Finally it was Vincent's turn.

'Now, Vincent! *What* have we got for *you*?'

The needle on Vincent's thrill-o-meter nudged past Christmas again.

Rupert smiled and flicked through his bookings book. Vincent was amazed he wasn't the slightest bit grumpy or weary after dealing with such fussy guests.

'Hmm. What about the Edible Rrr-room?' he suggested brightly. Vincent did appear in need of a good feed. His legs were so skinny they looked as if he'd swallowed two whole apples and they'd got stuck – right where his knees were meant to be. 'The carpet comes in chewy caramel or cookies 'n' cream and you can select sweet or savoury walls, whatever you prefer. You can lick, lick, lick away! And the peanut-butter lampshades and never-melting chocolate couch are to-die-for delicious, trust me. Or if you're after a bit of excitement, what about the Experiments Rrr-room? You can blow things up to your heart's delight in there. Or our Tiny Creatures Rrr-room? There's mice, pygmy possums, baby hedgehogs, chipmunks, hamsters. Or how about the International Space Station Rrr-room? The actual view from the Station is beamed down onto all four walls, which means sixteen sunsets and sunrises every day! And you're weightless of course. Except in the bathroom. That'd just be too tricky. Or one of my favourites, the Velcro Rrr-room. You can walk up the walls and across the ceiling – it's fabulous fun! And very practical too if you don't like hanging up your clothes or you tend to lose things. You just throw everything against the wall.'

Vincent looked wide-eyed at Rupert.

'How can I possibly choose between sixteen sunsets and peanut-butter flavoured lampshades?' he said. 'I'd like to stay in every single *one* of those rooms.'

'Or combine them all into one! Wouldn't THAT be grand? As long as you didn't blow up any tiny creatures I think it's a marvellous mix. I'll look into it.' Rupert scribbled a note in his bookings book. 'But for now, if your heart's no help, can I suggest a process of logical elimination?'

Vincent followed Rupert's advice. 'Okay, Florence

did mention buffet breakfast and something about chocolate fountains. So I guess I should rule out the Edible Room. I definitely don't want to miss out on chocolate fountains because I've stuffed myself with too much caramel carpet.' Vincent reminded himself that just two days ago he was dreaming of a bag of salt-and-vinegar chips and a sports drink and NOW he was turning down an entire edible room. Next Vincent eliminated the International Space Station Room. While he couldn't quite believe he was about to pass up the opportunity to fly right around the Earth every ninety minutes, he'd never dreamt of being an astronaut so perhaps now wasn't the time to start. Given his track record in science he felt it best to steer clear of the Experiments Room. It had taken almost two months for his eyebrows to grow back after his last efforts. Which left the Velcro Room and the Tiny Creatures Room.

'This is impossible!'

Rupert knew too much choice – for someone who never had any – could be decidedly not grand indeed. 'I've got it!' he announced. 'How about the Puppy Rrr-room? Basically you'll just be sleeping with all our leftover pocket dogs. There's at least another fifty who don't have a nice warm guest to cuddle up to tonight. So you'd be doing us a favour. And someone from front desk comes and takes them all out for a pee before you turn in.'

The red needle on Vincent's thrill-o-meter smashed through Christmas and pinged off into the universe somewhere. It felt like yet another scoop of ice-cream had been plonked on top of his towering cone. He wondered just how many scoops he could take before the whole thing toppled over.

A whole night with a roomful of pocket dogs! 'I'll take it!' he said.

'Wonderful.' Rupert tinkled the call-for-a-pony bell.

'Vincent,' came a voice from behind.

He turned to see Florence strolling towards him, piano and violin music wafting out of her flashing emerald boots. 'How was the tour?'

'Unbelievable! The whole place . . . completely unbelievable!'

'Have you chosen a room?'

'I'm in the Puppy Room.'

'Oh yay! The pocket dogs hate sleeping alone. They end up causing all sorts of mischief in the lobby if no one takes them. Emerson and I can take you there.'

Emerson was Florence's pocket dog. Upon hearing her name, she poked her head out of Florence's jacket and looked around.

'Brilliant!' enthused Rupert. 'And don't forget to call your mum, Vincent. Oh, that rrr-reminds me, Florry, your mum called. She can't Skype tonight.'

'Oh.' A look of disappointment darkened Florence's face. 'Did she say why?'

'She's having dinner with the Rrr-russian President. Apparently he got all cranky when she gave him a Hawaiian shirt as a gift. Turns out he doesn't like wearing shirts. And definitely not Hawaiian ones. She needs to get him back on side so they can find an Amur leopard for the Gene Bank.'

'I thought they were in Istanbul?'

'They were. They've had to fly to Rrr-russia specially, just for the dinner. There's no getting out of it, I'm afraid.'

'Of course. Never mind,' said Florence, trying to sound as if she didn't.

Florence and Vincent headed off across the lobby to the elevator.

'What's a Gene Bank?' asked Vincent. He thought it must have something to do with the expedition Florence's parents had embarked on three years ago.

'Oh. It's a project my mother and father came up with to save all the world's endangered species from extinction.'

'How will they do that?'

'Well, they have to gather tissue samples from every endangered animal on the planet. And then cryogenically freeze them.' Florence pushed the up button for the elevator. 'Then if they become extinct in the future, they can be cloned and brought back to life.'

'That's incredible,' marvelled Vincent.

'That's the easy part. Convincing governments around the world to cooperate is far trickier. Only half are on board so far. Thank goodness I have Rupert to help me or I don't know what I'd do.' Florence clicked the heels of her boots together like good-luck charms. After his grand tour, Vincent found it even more difficult to believe that Florence had been left to run the entire hotel by herself – even if she was a Wainwright-Cunningham.

As the elevator doors opened, Vincent just managed to stop his tongue doing the defrosted steak thing.

The elevator was as big as his entire house.

In the middle was a woman playing a grand piano.

'Zelda,' said Florence, stepping inside. 'This is Vincent. He's doing his orientation today and tomorrow he starts work as our shoeshine boy.'

Zelda looked up as her fingers danced gracefully across the keys. 'Hello, Vincent,' she said, smiling warmly. 'Welcome to The Grand.' With her head wrapped in a tall colourful turban and large gold earrings swinging from her ears, Vincent thought Zelda looked like a majestic African queen.

Without so much as a clunk the elevator, the size of a small house, began to rise. Zelda's playing was exquisite. More soothing than gentle rain. Vincent thought if Thom had a chance to pick any room at The Grand, he'd surely choose the elevator.

'Zelda's been with us for fifty years, haven't you?' said Florence.

'That's right, dear.'

'And she's never missed a day's work.'

Zelda laughed. 'Well, I have missed one, dear. My wedding day when I married Dr Maaboottee. But that was long before your time. In fact our anniversary is coming up soon.'

'Zelda's husband, Dr Maaboottee, works with us too. He's in charge of the elephants,' explained Florence. 'Oh, you have to celebrate, Zelda!'

'Just being married to Dr Maaboottee is enough of a celebration for me.' Zelda's fingers danced a little livelier across the keys as she thought about her beloved husband.

'When does Dr Maaboottee expect Winnie to give birth?' asked Florence. 'It feels like she's been pregnant forever.'

'I know, dear. Two years is a terribly long time to wait, but she still has a few months to go. Think how poor old Winnie must feel.'

'Who's Winnie?' asked Vincent.

'She's one of our elephants,' explained Zelda.

'I'm *so* excited,' cried Florence, clapping her hands together and springing up onto her toes. 'There really is nothing grander than a baby elephant.'

'When did you say your wedding anniversary is again?' asked Florence as they stepped out onto the eleventh floor.

'I didn't!' laughed Zelda.

'Come on, Zelda,' pleaded Florence, trying to keep the doors open a little longer.

'Goodbye, Florry.' The doors closed and the gentle piano music sunk down below.

'Hmm, she's not getting away with it *that* easily,' said Florence as they headed off down the corridor.

'Rupert will know, I'm sure. We never miss a chance to celebrate at The Grand, Vincent.'

As soon as Florence opened the door to the Puppy Room, a wave of pocket dogs crashed over them. Some were fluffy, others not, but all of them were impossibly cute in the way that tiny animals just are.

Lying on the floor, playing with the dogs, Florence and Vincent yakked away like old friends.

Turns out they had oodles in common.

Both of them loved a game of poker and a bet with Monopoly money. Both of them loved cheese on pizza but hated cheese sandwiches. Both of them knew every word to rapper MZee's 'Too Loose'. And they couldn't believe it when they discovered that both their dads had the same middle name – Benjamin! Although the chances were stacked in their favour since Florence's dad had twenty-three middle names, which Florence agreed was excessive, even for a grand person.

As a blood-orange light seeped in through the windows, one by one the pocket dogs curled up and fell asleep, like balls of fluffy wool scattered across the floor.

'I better go. I've left my glasses somewhere and I'll

have to retrace my steps till I find them. Why don't you call room service, Vincent? You look pooped.'

'Can I?'

'Of course! Order whatever you want.'

Room service! Another scoop!

Vincent had never ordered room service.

Obviously. He'd never stayed in a hotel!

Instead room service was a game he used to play with his mother before Thom came along. He would jump into her bed and she would knock on the door and say 'Room service'. And then she'd come in with his dinner on a tray and sit beside him while he ate it in bed. He felt like a king! Of course these days she was far too tired to play such games. She just focused on getting through dinner without having to clean food off the walls.

'All right. Where's the menu?' asked Vincent.

'There isn't one. You just order whatever you want.'

Boy oh boy! Vincent hopped between sleeping dogs over to the phone. 'Ah, could I please order one chicken pie, a pork chop with crackling, a bag of salt-and-vinegar chips, garlic bread, a bowl of hot chips and a caramel pudding with chocolate ice-cream and popcorn on top?'

'Of course. Any drinks, sir?'

'Ah, a smoking raspberry soda please. Actually, make that two.' Vincent had no idea what made the smoking sodas smoke – how's that for a tongue twister? – but he couldn't get enough of them.

Vincent dipped his last now-cold hot chip in a bit of popcorn and melted ice-cream and sat back against a wall of the softest pillows. Min was curled up on his tummy, which was so full he looked like he'd swallowed a bowling ball.

Trying not to disturb her, he reached across for the phone and called home.

Thom was screaming in the background. 'Vincent!' his mother yelled over the din. 'How is it?'

'It's amazing! You won't believe this place. I've got my own pock–'

'I'm sorry, I can't hear a word you're saying,' interrupted his mother. 'Can you talk a bit louder?'

'POCKET DOG! I'VE GOT MY OWN POCKET D–'

'It's no good, I can't hear you. I'll have to go and put some music on for Thom before he wakes your sister. I can't deal with tantrums *and* movie stars at this time of night. I'm glad you're having a good time, Vincent.'

Vincent and his mum yelled their goodbyes and hung up. He felt terrible that everyone at home was dealing with one of Thom's tantrums while he cuddled his very own pocket dog and sucked back smoking sodas. But there was another part of Vincent that didn't feel bad at all. In fact he felt a bit glad. Vincent tried not to visit that part of himself very often, but it wasn't always easy.

The dogs arrived back from their evening piddle and Vincent got ready for bed. He began the fiddly business of extracting Rose's eyebrow hairs from his toothbrush. He brushed his teeth and pulled his pyjamas out of his bag. A small package the size of a matchbox fell onto the bed. There was a note on top. Vincent took the rubber band off and read it. 'For big tim movie prowdusers.' It was a stack of homemade business cards.

Marilyn Montgomry
Versetile, dramatic actres
Can play leeding ladys or baddies

While Thom had knocked the dreams out of his parents, there was no knocking the dreams out of Rose! She'd wrapped herself up in dreams, just like her cape. *There's no way Rose would go to bed on her only night at The Grand.* Rose never wanted to go to bed full stop. 'The night is for stars,' she would say, 'and *I* am a WHOPPING BIG STAR!'

If I go to sleep, my day as a guest at The Grandest Hotel on Earth will be over. Rose is right. Not about those stars but real stars. This might be my one and only chance to see a falling star. Or those golf balls on the moon!

Vincent found a plush, silk bathrobe in the bathroom. He carefully slid the sleeping Min into a pocket, slung the binoculars round his neck and headed off into the night.

CHAPTER 7

HOT CHOCOLATE
AFTER MIDNIGHT

It was exciting!

To be wandering around the hotel all by himself. At night! Vincent felt like a grown-up. He pushed the down button and heard twinkling, smoky piano music rise up the elevator shaft. Expecting to see Zelda, he was a little taken aback when the doors opened and he saw a man wearing an ill-fitted tweed suit and cap hunched over an upright piano.

'Oh!'

'Evening, boy, where you headed?' asked the piano man. 'The bar?' He let out a raspy, deep cough. '*Hweer hweer*', then thudded his chest, as if trying to dislodge a coin stuck in a snack machine.

Maybe I look grown-up too! Vincent adjusted his silky robe. 'No, sir,' he said in his deepest voice. 'I'm going to the lobby balcony to look at the stars.'

'You could of done that from your room.'

Vincent felt eleven again.

It was true. Like every room at The Grand, his had a large balcony that looked out across the plateau.

'I didn't think of that.'

The piano player resumed playing.

'Are you the night-time piano player?' asked Vincent.

'I am. I prefer the night. A lot of birds come to sleep under my cap. I don't get that in the day.'

Vincent looked hard at the man's cap. He tried to imagine birds asleep on his head. He wanted to ask if there were any birds under there right now. Or where they came from, but decided against it. He didn't want to look stupid. Perhaps night-shift elevator piano players always have birds asleep on their heads. What would he know?

Vincent arrived on the balcony. It was full of guests in silk robes reclining on lounges, eyes to their binoculars, staring at the night sky. As they released a chorus of 'oohs' and 'aahs', Vincent found an empty lounge and lay down. He gazed up at the Milky Way. It was so clear! A jagged scar of light and diamonds and dust that slashed the sky in two.

The balcony let off a collective 'Aah!'

Vincent grabbed his binoculars. He saw it. A falling star! His first-ever falling star! Sailing across the sky as if it was in no hurry whatsoever.

The balcony let off more 'oohs'.

Another! His second!

And they kept coming, one after the other! Vincent was thrilled.

After two smoking drinks and a bowl of what-ever-flavour-you-think-of balls, Vincent's eyelids began to droop. He knew he had better get some sleep if he was to be his best shoeshining self in the morning.

As he got up to go, everyone removed their binoculars and waved. 'Goodnight, compadre,' they said with an enthusiasm and warmth shared only by people who lay together beneath stars as they fell from space.

Walking back to his room Vincent felt so happy.

He enjoyed meeting the strange piano man as much as the stargazing. His only regret was when given the opportunity to taste any flavour he could think of, the only one he could come up with was cheese and bacon. He didn't even like cheese and bacon! With his mind now overflowing with wild and delicious flavour ideas, Vincent was probably about halfway down the hall before he realised something wasn't right.

The what room?

Hang on.

I don't remember that room.

Vincent doubled back.

The Let It Be Room?

He walked back towards the elevator.

The Infinity Room? The Last Bets Room? The Fancy Seeing You Here Room? What?

Vincent walked up and down the hall, looking for the Puppy Room.

Oh no! I must have got out on the wrong floor!

And then he saw something that made his brain pulse and surge and fly off into orbit.

The Mirrors of the Future Room.

What the heck? A fortune-telling room? What on earth . . .? How can a room tell your future?

Vincent wasn't even sure he believed in fortune-telling. *How can anyone possibly see the future if it hasn't happened yet?*

Vincent reached out and touched the door. An electric sensation shot up his spine. Questions only the future knew the answers to flooded his mind.

Will Thom ever speak?

Will he ever be normal?

Will our family go back to the way it was?

Will he ever know I'm his brother?

Vincent felt drawn to the room as if it was a strong magnet and he was the Tin Man, yet at the same time something told him not to hang around. So Vincent pulled himself away and back stepped it to the elevator. It had jangled his nerves something terrible to think the answers to those questions could possibly be behind that door. Or any door! *Could they?* Most of him thought it impossible but another part of him believed anything was possible at The Grand! Rooms where you can remember your baby memories . . . a junkyard of dreams. The whole place felt as full of grand mysteries as it was wonder and beauty. *Is there any sort of grand this hotel isn't?*

'Vincent?'

Vincent swung round. 'Florence?'

'What are you doing here?' she said, closing the door to the Fancy Seeing You Here Room.

'Oh . . . I-I must have got out on the wrong floor.' For some reason Vincent felt guilty, as if he'd been caught doing something he shouldn't.

'Oh my,' said Florence, sounding flustered. 'You should be careful, Vincent. It's easy to get lost round here, more so than you might think. The Grand's not like other hotels, you know.'

Not like other hotels was an understatement. Without ever having stepped foot in another hotel Vincent was sure of that.

Florence looked worried. 'Are you okay?' asked Vincent.

'Oh yes,' replied Florence, unconvincingly, 'of course! Just can't sleep, that's all. I'm a total insomniac lately. Maybe that's why I keep forgetting things. Fancy a hot chocolate in the Marshmallow Lounge? That usually does the trick.'

Sitting in a cosy booth that looked like a pair of giant marshmallows squished around a table, Vincent stirred a big mug of hot chocolate. 'You're so lucky to live in a hotel. You get to order room service, eat breakfast from a buffet . . .'

'I know,' replied Florence, 'everyone always tells me how lucky I am. Lucky, lucky, lucky.'

'Don't you feel lucky?' asked Vincent. 'I mean The Grand, it's paradise!'

'That's true. Which makes it worse.' Florence fiddled with the beads on her hand-stitched jacket.

'Makes what worse? What do you mean?' Vincent heaped two teaspoons of mini marshmallows into his mug.

'Well, I know my parents' work is important, but sometimes I just wish they were around to tuck me in at night instead of being off somewhere saving the world's poorest children from starvation or the mountain mist frog from extinction,' she confessed. 'How bad is that?'

Vincent didn't think it was bad at all. In fact he understood completely.

'I know exactly how you feel,' he said, stroking Min, who'd woken up and was now wrestling a marshmallow on the table. Then he told Florence all about Thom. How he never spoke and had terrible tantrums and ate nothing but eggs. 'I love Thom. He's my little brother. But sometimes I just wish our family could go back to the way it was before he was born. Sounds terrible when I say it out loud. I think my bad trumps your bad.'

'Nah. I reckon it's a tie.'

Vincent and Florence smiled at each other.

It felt good to talk.

'You know, you're the first person I've ever admitted that to,' declared Florence. 'I sound like such a spoilt brat.'

'Well, you're the first person I've ever spoken to about Thom. I never really talk about him. To anyone.'

'How come?'

Vincent could feel his eyes prickle and mist. 'I don't know. I just don't.'

Florence nodded, like she understood completely.

'Well, that makes me feel special, Vincent.'

Vincent stared at Min. He worried if he caught Florence's eye he might actually cry.

'And can I just say, the chefs in the kitchen are going to be so excited to hear about Thom!' exclaimed Florence.

'What?' Vincent was completely lost.

'Eggs. They're drowning in them.'

Florence explained The Grand's hens were so happy they laid twice a day, sometimes three times.

'The chefs are practically buried in them. That's why they make life-size meringue giraffes and swans. They can't bear to let them go to waste. Take home as many as you want. Please!'

Florence yawned.

Vincent yawned too. 'Sleepy?' he asked.

'Sleepy. Do you want to have breakfast tomorrow?' Florence looked at the clock on the wall. 'Make that today.'

'Okay, sure.' Vincent couldn't believe it was past midnight. No wonder he was exhausted. He couldn't wait to get into his big comfy bed full of pocket dogs.

'Perfect! If you get there before me, make sure to get a table near the windows.'

'Why?'

'That'd spoil the surprise. You'll see!'

CHAPTER 8

VINCENT'S FIRST DAY AS THE SHOESHINE BOY

Vincent woke to find a pocket dog asleep on his face and two either side of his head like earmuffs. He tried to move and realised his whole body was covered in them, like periwinkles on a seaside rock. He removed the one from his face – it was Min. Vincent gave her a kiss and squeezed her into a spot on his chest. He lay there, enjoying every last moment of being buried in pocket dogs on a gigantic, comfy bed. His mind rewound back through his strange but wonderful night-time adventure, and arrived at the Mirrors of the Future Room. He'd heard of people who claimed to see the future but a room? Could you really find out what things were going to happen before they happened? His mind buzzed like a mozzie zapper in a swamp.

Vincent's stomach growled. He was starving.

Buffet breakfast!

Ever since Florence had mentioned chocolate fountains, the buffet breakfast was one of the things Vincent was most excited about. He dug himself out from under his blanket of pocket dogs, showered and put on his clothes from yesterday. He looked at himself in the flashy mirror. He did the best he could with his ordinary hair. He tugged at his sleeves and tried tucking his shirt into his pants to see if he looked any smarter. He didn't. Vincent wished he looked a little less like a scruffy kid from Barry and a little more, well, grand. But there wasn't much he could do about that. It was still all so hard to believe. Today he was going to start work as the shoeshine boy at The Grandest Hotel on Earth. Whoever would have imagined such a thing!

Thank you, Grandpa! Thank you!

As he opened the door to head off for breakfast, Rupert arrived to collect the pocket dogs.

'Ah, Vincent! How exciting. Your first day working at The Grand. That makes you family.

Welcome to the family!' Rupert threw his arms into the air and gave Vincent a great big bear hug. 'Now give me a hand with all these pocket dogs, will you?'

Vincent and Rupert collected the pocket dogs and put them in the basket ready for the day's new arrivals. Vincent was still holding onto Min, but as they picked up the last dog he knew the time had come to say goodbye.

'Be good, Min,' he said, sounding like a loose string on a guitar. He gave her a kiss on the nose and put her into the basket.

Rupert gave him a look that seemed to say, 'Don't be daft!'

Rupert dug Min back out. 'Don't be daft!' he said. 'Everyone who works at The Grand has their own pocket dog. And a pair of binoculars. It's part of the uniform. We find a dog in the pocket and a handy set of binoculars helps keep the true meaning of grand in clear sight at all times.'

Well, I'm sure you know, modern reader, how Vincent felt.

Yet another scoop!

He began to wonder if that feeling of a towering ice-cream cone with never-ending scoops had something to do with the true meaning of grand that Rupert spoke of. Vincent put Min in his top pocket and, smiling like a laughing Buddha, headed off for the Breakfast Hall.

Standing at the entrance, Vincent took his time. Buffet breakfast at The Grand was a once-in-his-lifetime event and he wasn't about to rush it. He let his nose suck up the sweet smells of fresh coffee, melting chocolate, buttery croissants and crispy bacon. He surveyed the room. On the right-hand side he saw an orchestra, the conductor swooping and diving in full musical flight as trolleys piled high with fresh pastries trundled past. At the buffet tables he watched a small army of chefs toasting muesli, tossing omelettes, frying eggs and flipping pancakes. And then he spotted them. Surrounded by a forest of fruit sculptures tall as trees at the far end of the room. Three glorious fountains spurting milk, dark and white chocolate ten feet into the air. Vincent's tummy gurgled like a bucketful of farting frogs. He started to drool like a teething baby. *Well, there's absolutely NO WAY I'm having eggs!*

Like a greyhound let out of the gate, Vincent grabbed a plate, piled it high with pancakes and headed straight to the chocolate fountains. When he got there he saw Mr Peach and his granddaughter,

Lily. Dressed head to toe in sparkles, both of them were laughing like spotted hyenas as they tried to place their pancake stacks under the fountains without ending up looking like a pair of chocolate-coated jelly babies themselves. It was impossible not to notice how their sad eyes of yesterday now sparkled like their bathrobes. Vincent joined them. He shoved his stack under the milk-chocolate fountain then ladled a pile of fresh raspberries on the top.

Remembering Florence's instructions, Vincent sat down at a table near the tall arched windows.

'Morning.'

It was April and her mother sitting at the next table along.

'Morning,' replied Vincent. He was about to ask about the Baby Memories Room when a giraffe stuck its big head through the open window, reached down and nudged April.

Right off her chair!

April laughed hysterically. As she stared up at the giraffe with its dark eyes and beautiful long lashes, a look of wonder and pure happiness swept across her face. April's mother handed her a carrot. 'Hold it up, as high as you can, April.'

The giraffe wrapped its long licorice tongue around the carrot and reeled it back into its mouth. They all laughed as it rolled the carrot round and round in its cheeks as if it was chewing gum.

Then Vincent felt a warm blast of nostril air on the back of his neck, followed by a firm nudge. Obviously the word about a bucket of carrots on table thirty-two had been passed around and two more giraffes had arrived, looking for their orange treat. Vincent stretched up and stroked the giraffe's polygon-patterned neck and his soft, floppy hamburger-bun lips. Being up so close to such a magnificent creature was astonishing. *Whoever dreamt you up?* he thought. Vincent had never *seen* a giraffe let alone patted one. I probably don't need to tell you, modern reader, there was no zoo in Barry. The most exotic creature in Barry was Mr Bidge, a budgerigar who sat behind the counter at the hardware store. (It used to be the parrot at the pet store, but you already know how that story ends.)

Vincent wolfed down his pancake stack in no time. Since Florence was yet to arrive he headed back to the buffet for a plate of waffles. On the way he had to do a double take when he passed Max and his mother. Mrs Peters was reading the paper and sipping a cup of tea. She looked *completely* relaxed while Max was eating breakfast with the sort of impeccable manners only the queen bothered with nowadays. Vincent could hardly believe it! Was this the same boy who less than twenty-four hours ago swung from the chandelier and dreamt of doing unspeakable things with elephant poo? Yesterday he was a bag of jiggles and insults, but today there was a calmness about him. He picked up his teacup, pinky finger raised, and sipped without a single slurp. He didn't even scrape his fork on his teeth!

At another table Vincent spotted the D'Silvas. They were having breakfast with a guest who was still wearing his pyjamas. Vincent realised it was Mr Cash, the busy businessman. Despite the D'Silvas having turned their noses up at them yesterday, scampering about on the table were five pocket dogs running amok. The boys were feeding them bits of toast and bacon and pouring water into an empty butter dish so they could have a drink. Vincent scanned the table. Not a single phone in sight!

There was something *else* different about the D'Silvas too.

Aha, thought Vincent. *It's their ski-jump noses!*

Yesterday they were a steep black run and this morning they were more like a gentle beginner's slope. *But how is that possible?* Then again he was eating breakfast with a giraffe. How was anything at The Grand possible?

As he strained to get a better look, Rupert arrived at the D'Silvas' table.

'Ah morning, everyone! I see your midnight delivery of pocket dogs arrived safe and sound. *So* glad you changed your mind.' The three D'Silva boys agreed, and cooed at their fluffy friends in those high-pitched voices people use when they speak to babies. 'Ha wo, wittle fellwa! You da *cooooo*dest puppy ever, squidgy-midgey, give me a kissy!' The pocket dogs licked the D'Silva boys all over their faces.

'Ah, Rupert,' said Mr Cash, 'I've called the office. Turns out they can get by without me for a while, so I was wondering if I could extend my stay? Perhaps for a month? Maybe two?'

'Of course! Stay as long as you like. We never rrr-run out of rrr-rooms at The Grand.'

'No work for a month. That sounds like a cause for celebration. Maybe we should stay too!' said

Mr D'Silva, wildly. He stood up and threw his arms in the air. 'Champagne for everyone. On me!'

The breakfast room erupted in cheers.

Mr D'Silva sat back down again. 'Just whack it on my bill, will you, Rups, and make sure it's the good stuff!'

'Of course, Mr D'Silva.'

'And what time did you say those sloth classes were on again?' inquired Mr Cash.

'"Find Your Inner Sloth" classes start sometime around three. But they often begin late – as you'd expect. Sloths are not known for punctuality,' said Rupert.

Everyone laughed – Mr and Mrs D'Silva, their three boys and Mr Cash.

'Rrr-right you are then! Everything seems to be going grandly.' Rupert rubbed his hands together with glee. 'I'll be at the front desk if you need anything. Enjoy your day, everyone.'

Rupert loved nothing more than happy guests. He sashayed off, back stepping and leaping every few metres or so as if he had a dance bottled up inside and someone had given him a mighty good shake.

'Morning. Sorry I'm late, Vincent.' Florence sat down with two slices of tomato toast and a cup of tea. 'The Aquatic Room sprung a leak. The plumber's only just found it.'

Vincent, with a mouthful of waffle, made a noise that sounded like 'moew-ring'. A bit of chewed up blueberry fell onto his plate.

Florence laughed. 'You remembered!'

'Mer-rembered what?' (My co-author has requested I don't describe what Vincent's mouth full of chewed up blueberry waffle looked like and I have agreed.)

'A window table! It's just not breakfast at The Grand if you don't get dribbled on by a giraffe.'

Vincent smiled. He let out a loud, grumbly burp. '*BWERP!*'

Florence sniffed the air. 'Blueberry and elder-flower! My favourite. Looks like you're getting the hang of The Grand.'

Florence had barely a bite of her tomato toast before declaring she needed to get cracking. She took a slurp of tea. 'Come on, I'll show you where you're working.'

When they reached the lobby Florence took Vincent by the arm. 'Close your eyes.'

Vincent could hear the excitement in her voice. He felt it too, mixed in with a good dose of first-day nerves.

'Okay, you can look now.'

Vincent opened his eyes.

He was stunned. Expecting to see a small space where he could set down his box and stool, instead he saw a luxurious, specially designed red shoeshine chair. Sitting on a platform so the shoe mounts were just the right height for polishing shoes, Vincent thought it looked fit for a king!

Florence ran to the wall and flicked a switch. Above the chair, a large green neon sign buzzed on: SHOESHINE it said, and dangling from the last 'E' were a pair of neon boots.

She clambered up onto the platform and sat in the chair. 'What do you think?'

Vincent put down his Pa's box and stool. 'Wow! It's so . . . grand.'

Vincent marvelled at the chair. It was so beautiful and cleverly designed he worried if his shoeshining skills would be impressive enough to match it.

'Oh, I almost forgot,' said Florence, racing off. She returned carrying a large bag over her arm.

'What's that?' he asked.

'Have a look.'

Vincent unzipped the bag and pulled out a bright blue suit.

'Oh my goodness,' he whispered, 'a suit.'

'It's your uniform. Look at the pockets,' insisted Florence.

Above the right top pocket and stitched in red running writing was Vincent's name. And in the left was a special The Grandest Hotel on Earth notepad and pen.

'For orders. And all those wonderful shoe design ideas you told me about.'

Vincent was speechless.

'Have a look at the back.'

He twirled the jacket round. Embroidered in yellow and white was a magnificent scene of the hotel surrounded by snow-capped mountains and beneath it the hotel catchphrase: '*Everyone deserves a bit of grand.*'

'Put it on!' said Florence, excitedly.

Beside the chair Vincent had his own bathroom. He took off his clothes and slipped on the suit. It was a perfect fit. Vincent had never worn a suit before. He barely recognised himself. He ran his hands down the sleeves that went all the way to his wrists. The material was so soft and luxurious.

'Come out,' cried Florence. So Vincent did. 'Wow! You look like a million bucks!'

And he felt it too. Before putting on his uniform he had been ordinary, eleven-year-old Vincent from Barry. But now he felt completely different. Suddenly he felt like someone important. Suddenly he was the shoeshine boy at The Grandest Hotel on Earth!

Vincent wanted to do a good job so badly. He stood up tall, straight as he could beside his red leather chair. Standing up straight was somehow easier in a suit.

'I guess I'll just wait for my first customer.'

'How about you practise on me! My boots are always in need of a polish,' suggested Florence, diving back into the chair. She had a million other things to do, but right now she was having so much fun. She'd forgotten what it was like to have a friend her own age.

Vincent rummaged around in his pa's box and to his surprise he immediately found a pot of emerald polish – *exactly* the same green as Florence's boots. It seemed there was no end to the magic of his pa's shoe-cleaning kit.

'These are amazing!' said Vincent, turning Florence's boots over in his hands.

'I know. I don't think I could do my job without

them. Bach and flashing lights somehow make everything seem possible.'

Vincent removed the lights and checked each and every bulb was working. He examined the electrical circuits and rewired one of the speakers in the heel. And then he polished and brushed the boots till they shined like new.

As Vincent applied the finishing touches, another guest arrived with a pair of trainers in desperate need of some love and for the rest of the day Vincent was so busy he barely had time to look up. He polished guests' shoes and boots till they gleamed like new. He repaired their favourite high heels and put the bounce and pizzazz back into the fanciest of sneakers. He even found a spray in his grandfather's box that got rid of foul odours and made every pair of shoes smell so good you'd be happy to drink soup out of them.

CHAPTER 9

NOT THE BEST GLASSES

When Vincent arrived home, he couldn't wait to tell his family all about The Grand and his first day as a shoeshine boy.

Rose was sitting in the gutter out the front with cottonwool between her toes and a pot of bright red nail polish.

'Hi Rose, I mean, Marilyn.'

She groaned a long theatrical groan, then rolled her eyes back into her head till they were nothing but white. The whole world was a stage to Rose, even the gutter.

'What's up?'

'I'm *sick* of classical music, that's what. It's been

going *all* day. It's *not* fair. I *never* get to listen to my music EVER.'

'Is Thom having a bad day?'

Rose screwed up her nose. 'Does he have good ones? Mum tried to get him to eat spaghetti. I don't know why she doesn't just give up. He's never going to eat anything but eggs.'

'What did he do?'

'Oh, you know. The usual,' said Rose, painting her toenails and trying to sound as if she didn't care. 'He chucked the bowl of spaghetti at the wall and then climbed up on top of the kitchen cupboards and threw Mum's best glasses onto the floor.'

'Not the wedding ones from Aunty Ada?'

'Yep. Then she yelled at me to go outside in case I got glass in my feet. If you go in there now, she'll probably yell at you too. Better stay out here. Then you can't get into trouble.' Rose leapt to her heels, toes in the air so as not to wreck the polish. 'Anyway, I don't want to talk about *Thom*. Did you meet any big-time movie producers? Did you give them my card?'

'No, but I met an eagle hunter from Mongolia. His eagle was this big!' Vincent held his hands out to show Rose how big. 'He held it in his arms like

112

a sleeping baby while I repaired the yak fur inside his boots!'

Rose looked unimpressed. 'What about movie stars? Did you meet any of those?'

'No. But I did fix crampon spikes for a scientist from Antarctica who . . .'

Rose's attention evaporated at 'no'. She thought a scientist from Antarctica was about as interesting as an end-of-year assembly when they hand out the awards to the same kids who *always* get the awards. BORING!

'Vincent!' He turned to see his dad walking down the street. 'How did you go?'

'Dad!' Vincent ran and gave his father a hug. 'It's unbelievable. It's like an African game park meets Disneyland meets Shangri-la!' Not that Vincent had been to an African game park or Disneyland or Shangri-la, obviously.

'Great,' scowled Rose. 'I'm stuck at home, listening to rubbish Shostakovich for the ten-millionth time and you're in African Disneyland.' She pulled her cape up and over her head. 'This is going to be the LONGEST BUMMER SUMMER EVER.'

SMASH!

'THOM!'

The three of them turned towards the house.

'Sounds like your mother needs me.'

Vincent's father looked weary as he walked up the front steps and went inside.

Vincent followed.

Rose started counting. 'One, two, three, four, five . . .'

'DON'T COME IN HERE, VINCENT! YOU'LL JUST SPREAD GLASS ALL THROUGH THE HOUSE. GO OUTSIDE, WILL YOU!'

Vincent walked back outside.

'Told you.'

He sat down on the front steps and wondered how many more hours till he could return to The Grandest Hotel on Earth. The Mirrors of the Future Room glowed in his mind's eye like his neon shoeshine sign. He wanted to know if that room really could answer those questions. He wanted to know if the way his family had become was the way his family would always be. Right now, if the room could tell him, Vincent thought he'd walk right in.

CHAPTER 10

A GRAND FAMILY

Every morning, Vincent could barely wait to get back to the hotel. He flew out of bed, dressed in seconds, ate breakfast on the run and brushed his hair on the bus. Everyone who worked at The Grand was treated like family and what a wonderful big family it was. There were twenty-seven back scratchers, thirty-nine professional flyswatters, ninety-three pooper-scoopers, forty chefs, twenty bakers, ten chocolatiers, ninety-seven window cleaners, thirteen zoologists, two cobweb hunter and removers (they never destroyed a web, just moved it elsewhere), nine mechanics, twenty-eight foot masseurs, twelve dog walkers, one herpetologist who took care of the turtles and the lizards in the Lizard Lovers Room, seventy-seven gardeners, fifty sweet souls who turned down the beds at night and left chocolates on the pillows, fifty-eight comedians, three lepidopterists who looked after the butterflies, one sloth master – 'cause quite frankly sloths can take excellent care of themselves, seven professional card and backgammon players, nineteen baby whisperers, fourteen wilderness experts, thirty-two sets of willing-to-stand-in grandparents, one-hundred-and-one wandering minstrels, fifty baristas, four full orchestras and nine professional huggers. And then of course there was Florence and Rupert and Zelda and Dr Maaboottee. And now, Vincent.

According to Florence *everyone* who worked at The Grand was valued equally for their particular skill. But far and away the most famous workers were the lobby cleaners – Luz and Tracee. You see Luz and Tracee had discovered that the best way to clean the lobby was to slide across it at high speed with rags on their feet. Or dance. For one, it was much less boring that way, and two, they covered a lot of floor quickly. They were always up to date on the very latest styles. And at night they held dance classes in the Transatlantic Ballroom where they taught guests how to 'crump' and do the 'signal the plane' or the 'throw them bones'. The most popular new dance at The Grand was the 'living my best life'. And it had taken the place by storm. Everywhere you went you'd see guests doing it, staff doing it. Even Vincent had caught the bug. Between customers, he'd be practising away, giving the 'living my best life' a red-hot crack.

Luz and Tracee were such a hit the hotel printed a range of instructional dance step postcards. They sold like hotcakes as every guest clambered to take a slice of hotel life back into their own. And when it came time for guests to leave, it had become a tradition at The Grand for Luz and Tracee to dance them off. The lobby band would start up and every farewell turned into something more like a wild party – which had the added bonus of stopping guest farewells becoming weepy affairs.

'I don't know how you do it but my shoes and the boys' sneakers have never looked so good,' said Mr D'Silva, hopping out of the chair. 'Here's an extra twenty for you, son.'

'Thanks, Mr D'Silva.' Vincent tucked the tip into his shoebox.

'You know sneakers are as valuable as gold these days. My boys are more attached to their shoes than their phones. And they certainly have more of them! You could make a fortune selling that polish stuff of yours.'

'You mean my Kick-easy Sneaker Shield Gel? I'd never thought of that, Mr D'Silva.'

'Well, you should. We're headed home today. Here's my card. If you ever need some money to get started, give me a call.'

Mr D'Silva headed off to the front desk to check out. After shifting from *La Chambre de Pommes Frites*, the D'Silvas had spent a night in the Butterfly Room, the Everyone Sings Sweetly Room and the Stephen Hawking Room before ending their stay in the African Sky Room. Apparently the dung beetles and the D'Silvas got along fine although Mrs D'Silva did enquire if one could be made into a brooch as a souvenir.

Apart from Mr Cash, who'd set up camp with the sloths on Fin's Island, Vincent noticed all the guests he did orientation with were checking out to leave. The three D'Silva boys were bent over the lobby balcony, peacefully birdwatching with their binoculars, while pocket dogs tumbled around their feet. Max was sitting in the armchair he'd used to swing from the chandelier, reading a fat book of poetry while his mother and Mrs D'Silva were exchanging phone numbers. April, surrounded by sleeping dogs, was sitting on the floor, brushing her pony's tail. Vincent pulled out some inserts he'd made to help with her wobbly walk and headed over.

'Hi April,' he said. 'I wanted to give you these before you go. I thought they might help you walk a little easier.'

'That's very kind of you, Vincent,' said April's mother. She took off April's shoes and slipped the jelly-like inserts inside.

April stood up. Her mother hovered by her side, arms outstretched in case she fell. April took a step. Then another. A huge smile lit up her face. 'Wow!' declared April. 'The ground's stopped moving.' She strode across the lobby. 'Look, Mumma! I'm walking! By myself!'

Vincent watched as April walked around the fountain and back again. He had that same tingly feeling he felt after his first satisfied customer at Barry Train Station.

Back at his chair, Vincent pulled out his notepad

and set to work designing a pair of shoes so that April could run. *Everyone loves to run!*

As he scribbled away, Chelsea came over to say goodbye.

'Hi Chelsea. All packed and ready to go?' Vincent reached out and patted Jess, the shaggy black-and-white pup he had first set his sights on.

'Yes, um, I just want to apologise for snatching Jess off you,' said Chelsea, sheepishly.

'Oh, that's okay.' Vincent looked down at Min, whose head was poking out of his top pocket. 'I ended up with Min so how could I be angry about that?'

'Well, that's nice of you to say, but it was pretty poor form.' Chelsea reached out and patted Min. 'Sometimes this bad feeling just comes over me and I get so . . .'

'Angry?'

'Yes. Angry. And then I just want what everyone else has. I can't really explain it.' Chelsea looked up at the midnight-blue ceiling. 'It doesn't make sense but I think it's because I miss my mum.'

Vincent didn't know what had happened to Chelsea's mum, but he did understand the feeling. Sometimes he felt angry about how much time his mum spent with Thom.

'Can you take a picture of me and Dad?' she asked.

'Sure.' Chelsea ran across the lobby to get her dad who was busy buying Luz and Tracee postcards. They wrapped their arms around each other and squeezed one another tight for the photograph. Chelsea's dad's droopy eyes lifted and flashed with happiness.

The lobby band started playing the 'living my best life' song. 'Come on, Dad, dance with me.'

Vincent lined up with Rupert and Florence, ready to dance everyone off. He watched April wiggle her hips and shuffle and laugh. He felt proud as a peacock. As they stuck out their butts and shook their shoulders, Vincent saw Rupert wipe a tear from his eye.

'Are you okay?' asked Vincent.

'Oh, don't mind me. I always cry at departures.'

Vincent realised Luz and Tracee's dance offs were just as much for the people who worked at the hotel as those who came to stay.

Florence and Vincent stood on the balcony as the last guests trotted off on their llamas to catch the hot air balloon.

'I don't know about you, but I could murder a tomato sandwich. How about lunch?' said Florence.

121

Eating together had become a regular thing for Vincent and Florence. Usually followed by a race or two around the rocking-horse racetrack. Rocking-horse races really were the silliest thing but ridiculously fun.

'We could eat at the Elephant House if you like, see how Winnie's doing?' suggested Florence.

'I don't know about a tomato sandwich, but I wouldn't mind peanut butter. I just have one pair of sandals to finish. Meet you there in ten?'

When Vincent arrived at the Elephant House, Florence was leaning against the enclosure fence watching Dr Maaboottee cut Winnie's toenails with a machete.

'Is she bigger or am I imagining it?' asked Florence.

'Do you mean is she bigger than yesterday – the last time you asked? No, I don't think so, Florry,' said Dr Maaboottee as he carefully shaved off a bit more toenail.

'I *swear* she looks bigger!'

Dr Maaboottee gently rubbed Winnie's huge tummy. 'Perhaps it's because she's lying down. I'm afraid she has a fair way to go yet, Florry. No doubt Winnie is as keen for her baby to come as you are.'

Vincent and Florence climbed up onto the fence and unwrapped their sandwiches. As they ate, Vincent, who was usually quite chatty, stared off into the distance.

'You're quiet,' said Florence.

Vincent didn't respond.

She waved a hand in front of his eyes. 'Hello! Is anyone home?'

'Oh, sorry,' he said, blinking. 'Did you say something?'

'I said you're quiet.'

'Oh. Am I?'

'Yes. Let me guess, new ideas for shoes?'

'No, actually. I'm thinking about the guests who just left.' A thread of astonishment lit up Vincent's words.

'What about them?'

'Well, I mean, did you see the D'Silva boys? Their mum and dad had to drag them off the balcony. They didn't want to stop birdwatching!'

'I know,' replied Florence with a giggle. 'They left their phones behind too.'

'Does that always happen?' asked Vincent.

'People leaving their phones? Quite a lot actually.'

'No. Not the phones. It's just, everyone seemed

so completely different to the people they were when they arrived.'

'Ah, that. Yes, well, that's what The Grand's all about, Vincent.'

'What do you mean?'

'Oh, a bit of grand changes everything! It's positively transformational, as Rupert likes to say.'

Vincent found all this talk of 'a bit of grand' completely confusing. But at the same time, he'd just seen it with his own eyes.

'Does it always work?' he asked.

Florence shrugged and nodded. 'Almost always. Some of the rooms in this hotel are extremely powerful. That's why we have to be careful. Knowing who can handle them and who can't takes years of training. Put someone in the wrong room and you could end up doing more harm than good. My grandmother always said some changes in life are better left up to the gods, whoever they may be. And some things we can't change. All we're trying to do is give everyone a bit of grand. I know it doesn't always look like it, but we take what we do here very seriously. Life can be terribly tough sometimes.'

Florence took a bite of her tomato sandwich while Vincent chewed over her words.

'Is that why people come here?'

'Hmm. That's a tricky question,' replied Florence. 'You see, most people don't choose to stay at The Grand, The Grand chooses them.'

Vincent slumped, crossing his arms. 'Huh?' Whatever understanding he thought he had about 'a bit of grand' disappeared like a white dove under a magician's handkerchief. 'How does it do that?'

'Well, to explain that properly I'd need more time than it takes to eat a tomato sandwich, which is all I've got spare today. But I can tell you it's not anything to do with being rich or poor, and all about who's in need. I'd better run.' Florence jumped down off the fence. 'Fin thinks baby Barbara has a gas problem. A sloth with nice breath is a bad sign. I've got a mammalogist arriving now. Bye, Dr Maaboottee. Bye, Winnie. See you later, Vincent.'

It was a lot to take in. As Vincent packed up for the day, his mind roamed over the guests who had arrived and the guests who had left and the incredible differences between the two. He mulled over the idea of a hotel choosing its guests instead of its guests choosing it. He had wanted to ask Florence about the Mirrors of the Future Room but something stopped him. What though, he had no idea. No wonder stories swirled around the place!

'Oh, tell me I'm not too late!' said a voice sounding like a cat caught in a drain.

Vincent looked up to see an elderly lady wearing a winged jumpsuit and a helmet getting out of the elevator. In her hands was a pair of small orange tap shoes. 'You wouldn't have time to give my grand-daughter's tap shoes a quick polish, would you, dear? She refuses to wear anything else, and she needs them for dinner.'

'Of course,' said Vincent.

'Oh, you are a lovely boy!' The old lady winked and handed Vincent the shoes. 'She's in the Synchronicity Room, level sixteen. Can you leave them outside the door when you're done? I'm off to the platform.' Vincent did his best not to look shocked. He didn't want to offend her but she looked ancient. Far too old to be jumping off the side of a mountain.

Vincent got to work on the tap shoes. First he checked the screws holding the metal taps in place. Next he mixed a number of colours together till he had the exact orange and then he brushed and polished them till they shined like the sun.

'Vincent!' said Zelda as he stepped into the elevator. 'How was your first week at The Grand?'

'Amazing,' said Vincent. 'It's hard to take it all in.'

'I'm sure it is. Now where to?'

'The sixteenth floor. I have to deliver these shoes for that old lady.'

Zelda stopped playing. Her huge hoop earrings seemed to swing by themselves. 'What old lady?'

'You must have seen her. She was wearing a winged jumpsuit and a helmet. She got out of the elevator about ten minutes ago.'

'Did you say level sixteen?'

Vincent nodded.

Zelda looked confused. 'I don't think we have any guests on sixteen at the moment.'

'Well, that's what she said. The Sin-chronee-city Room? Something like that. It ended in "city" anyway.'

Zelda pursed her lips into a concerned pout. 'If you say so.'

Vincent pushed the button for the sixteenth floor and Zelda resumed playing.

Without so much as a wobble, the elevator rose up and up and then stopped. *DING!*

'Just make sure you leave the shoes outside the room, Vincent,' said Zelda as the elevator doors opened. 'You should never wander into rooms willy-nilly. No point looking for trouble.'

'I won't.'

'Remember. We can undo things, but we can never unsee them.' A deep note of unease swung from her words.

Vincent nodded again and Zelda's hands returned to the piano, gambolling across the keys like children in a playground.

CHAPTER 11

THE SIXTEENTH FLOOR

Vincent stood for a moment staring at the elevator. Zelda had been so serious. She was usually warm and friendly. Vincent was beginning to realise there was a lot more to The Grand than he first thought. It wasn't just some wildly luxurious hotel. There were other things going on. Things he didn't understand. He remembered what Florence had said at lunch, about powerful rooms and transformations. He thought about the D'Silva boys and Max and Chelsea. The more he thought about everything, the more confused he felt.

Vincent headed down the hall and quickly found the Syn-chronee-city Room.

He stood outside the door.

Inside his mind questions flew like arrows across a battlefield.

I wonder why they're in the Synchronicity Room? What's in there? What does synchronicity mean? Could it be an exact replica of a city called Syn-chronee, which they had to flee?

Vincent touched the gold letter 'S' with his finger.

He desperately wanted to knock and hand the tap shoes over in person. That way he could catch a glimpse of the room and the guests as well.

He clenched his hand into a fist and went to knock on the door.

But then he stopped himself.

He remembered the look on Zelda's face and what she had said about looking for trouble.

Vincent put the tap shoes down outside the door. He turned and walked back up the hall towards the elevator.

But when he got there, he didn't stop. Instead, he kept right on walking. *I wonder what rooms are up this end?*

Vincent passed the Infinity Room, the Alchemy Room, the Last Bets Room . . . the Fancy Seeing

You Here Room. The fact he had seen these rooms before didn't register until he saw it – the Mirrors of the Future Room. Vincent cursed himself. Of all the rooms to be standing in front of after Zelda's words of warning. That was the downside to being treated like family. Your best behaviour is more prone to slip when you feel right at home.

Vincent looked up and down the corridor. There was no one around. He shut his eyes, hoping his huge dilemma might disappear. But when he opened them, everything was exactly the same as it was before.

Vincent told himself to turn and go back to the elevator.

Am I seriously going to mess up my first week at The Grandest Hotel on Earth, the most incredible thing that's ever happened to me?

It was true. Vincent hadn't been this happy in a long time.

So he mustered all his strength and managed to take one step away from the room. *Yes! Now do it again!*

Vincent took another step. *Yes!*

Slowly, step by step he walked backwards until he reached the elevator and, before giving himself a chance to double think, he slammed his hand onto the down button.

The ring around it lit up.

He was safe.

Zelda would be here any minute.

Vincent stood there, his heart pounding as the strains of Beethoven's all-knowing ninth symphony rose up the elevator shaft.

CHAPTER 12

THE MIRRORS OF THE FUTURE ROOM

It was only a day or so later when Vincent found himself on the extremely strange sixteenth floor for the third time.

And to be fair, what happened wasn't entirely Vincent's fault.

Vincent was packing up for the day – just like last time – when the old woman wearing a winged jumpsuit and helmet – just like last time – asked Vincent if he could clean her granddaughter's tap shoes – just like last time. And if Vincent would be good enough to deliver the shoes to their room on – you guessed it – the sixteenth floor.

Just.

Like.

Last.

Time.

Only this time the room was different. Instead of the Synchronicity Room they were now staying in the Room of Beautiful Coincidences.

Standing next to Zelda's grand piano, Vincent told himself he was going to go straight to the room, leave the shoes outside the door and get off the sixteenth floor as fast as he could. But when he found the Room of Beautiful Coincidences, Vincent's heart beat so fast his rib cage rattled. I'm sure every modern reader has already guessed why. The Room of Beautiful Coincidences was right next to which room?

That's right.

The Room of Beautiful Coincidences was right next to the Mirrors of the Future Room.

Vincent put the shoes down outside the door.

But being so close to the Mirrors of the Future Room, in no time at all Vincent's desire to know Thom and his family were going to be okay had thrown a great big sheet over his best intentions so Vincent couldn't find them. Then it threw a great big sheet over Zelda's and Florence's words of warning so he momentarily forgot them. Then his desire to know Thom and his family were going to be okay threw a great big sheet over itself and disguised itself as reason. A bit like that wolf who dressed up as Little Red Riding Hood.

A peek can't hurt, reasoned Vincent – or, more accurately, fooled himself. *It's not like I'm going to go in. I'll just open the door a tiny bit.*

(My co-author just ran out of the room. Says he can't stand the tension.)

Vincent knocked lightly on the door.

Silence.

He knocked again, slightly louder this time.

Again. Nothing.

He put his hand around the doorknob.

And left it there.

His heart pounded.

His hand began to sweat, making the metal doorknob feel ice cold. He double-checked no one was around and then slowly turned it to the right. Unexpectedly, the bolt popped out of the lock and the door moved into the room. He quickly wrenched it back towards him.

What the heck! It's like it wants me to open it.

Or so he told himself.

Knowing the door could pop open easily, Vincent wiped his sweaty palms on his pants and gripped the doorknob more firmly. Then, as carefully as he could, he turned it to the right again. He heard the click as the bolt popped out of the lock. Now the only thing holding the door shut was Vincent's hand. He was holding the doorknob so tightly his hand started to shake. Trying to keep it steady, he inched the door into the room until a slender crack of light appeared.

Vincent closed his left eye and put his right eye up to the crack.

It took a moment for his vision to bend the light and pull focus.

A sliver of room came into view.

It looked like an ordinary – albeit grand – hotel room. The bed was exactly the same as the Puppy Room. The bedside lamp too. Above the bed hung a painting of the Mabombo Ranges. Vincent strained to see more but it was impossible. To do so he would need to open the door a fraction wider. Without any further contemplation Vincent inched the door into the room until the crack was *twice* as big as it was before. He saw an armchair and an arched window that looked out onto the mountains. On the other side of the room he saw a half-open door leading into the bathroom. Vincent could see the sink and before he could stop himself he looked up and straight into the bathroom mirror.

Vincent felt a bolt of energy race up his spine and neck and into his head.

His brain blew a fuse.

His scalp and hair tightened and burned as if they were on fire.

Blue-white lightning flashed before his eyes.

Then, suspended in space, Vincent saw an image. It was a crouching elephant and a bald man with huge sunglasses playing piano.

Vincent yanked the door towards him and slammed it shut.

He felt freaked out and full of regret all at the same time.

Why did I do that? What have I done?

Vincent flew out of the elevator, ran into the bathroom next to his shoeshine chair and locked the door.

How could I have been so stupid? What will Florence and Zelda and Rupert think if they find out what I've done? They trusted me. Florence could have chosen anyone to be the shoeshine boy at The Grandest Hotel on Earth but she chose me. Me! Not anyone else. ME! And it's the best thing that has ever happened. Ever!

Vincent felt so ashamed. And what made everything worse was it had all been for nothing. He'd risked everything for nothing. The vision had zero to do with Thom. Or his family. A crouching elephant and a bald man with big glasses playing piano? It was like a bad joke! Perhaps it was? Or maybe the room was out of order? Maybe that's why Zelda had warned him? In which case what did that mean?

Vincent felt sick with guilt and nervous unknowing. He felt like throwing up. Now he would give anything to go back in time not forwards.

Knock, knock!

There was someone at the door!

'You in there, Vincent?'

It was Florence.

'Yes. I'm just getting changed.'

'Any chance you have time to squeeze in a lap of the rocking-horse racetrack before you head off?'

'Okay. I'll be out in a second.'

Vincent looked at himself in the mirror. 'I swear on my mum's and dad's graves, I'll NEVER open that door again! NEVER!'

138

CHAPTER 13

THE MAABOOTTEES' FIFTIETH WEDDING ANNIVERSARY

After the incident in the Mirrors of the Future Room, Vincent threw himself into his work. He worked harder and more diligently than ever before. It was almost like he believed if he brushed hard enough, he could scrub out what he had done. At the start of every day he reminded himself his job was to shine shoes. And he had *no* business doing anything else at The Grand *other* than *that*. As Vincent worked harder, his passion for shoes grew stronger. He invented special woven inserts using the llamas' wool that made the most uncomfortable high heels feel like walking barefoot on the softest carpet. He experimented with polishes, mixing them together till he could match the colour of any shoe *exactly*. And he came up with a way to make the creases in a worn-out pair of shoes disappear completely.

So one day when he went to deliver a pair of tightrope shoes to a tightrope walker on the ninth floor, he'd almost forgotten the Mirrors of the Future Room even existed.

'Morning, Zelda,' said Vincent. He pushed the button for the ninth floor and turned – as he always did – to have a chat. But the person sitting at the piano wasn't Zelda. The person sitting at the piano was wearing a velvet turquoise suit. He was also bald as a light bulb and had on ridiculously big sunglasses. The elevator doors closed and the lift began to climb.

'Oh, sorry! Where's Zelda?'

'No idea,' said the piano man. 'I just got a call a few weeks back booking me to play today.' And then he let out a familiar raspy cough. *HWER HWER!*

And then it struck Vincent.

It was him! Not the man with the head where birds slept – although it probably was him. This was the man he saw in the mirror!

Vincent watched the numbers light up as the elevator climbed towards the ninth floor. *What's going on? What does it mean?*

He remembered the other image. The crouching elephant. There were definitely no sleeping birds in the vision, just an elephant with back legs bent as if trying to kneel.

Ding! The elevator arrived at the ninth floor.

Ding! Suddenly the images made sense. It was Winnie! The elephant was Winnie! The elephant was crouching because it was giving birth. Today must be the day Winnie is going to have her baby.

Vincent almost fell out of the elevator. He sprinted down the corridor to the Huggle Room where the tightrope walker was staying, banged on the door, dropped the shoes and sprinted back to the elevator.

I've got to find Dr Maaboottee!

Vincent pushed the down button like a human jackhammer. His panic level rose as he watched the light flick slowly from one number to the next as the elevator descended. He hammered the down button some more.

What am I going to say?

Then the elevator stopped on the tenth floor. *What?*

Someone must be getting in or out. Cripes, I can't just stand here!

Vincent heaved open the heavy fire door and flew down the stairs. He burst out of the fire escape, into the lobby and raced over to the front desk – nearly falling over a pony – where Florence was busy checking in new arrivals.

'Excuse me, Florence,' said Vincent, trying to swallow his huffing and puffing and sound casual. 'Sorry to interrupt, I was just wondering if you knew where I could find Dr Maaboottee?'

'Oh, it's Dr Maaboottee and Zelda's fiftieth wedding anniversary today. I insisted they take the day off. We've arranged a picnic for them over in the next valley. And a special choir from Dr Maaboottee's home town to sing for them. He's going to love it!' declared Florence, obviously pleased as punch with the special event she'd planned. 'Didn't I tell you? We never miss a chance to celebrate at The Grand! They're leaving on the next hot air balloon. Oh look, here they come now. Shhh! Don't breathe a word. It's a surprise.'

Vincent turned to see Zelda and Dr Maaboottee dressed to the nines, their arms linked as they walked across the lobby.

Oh no! This is a disaster! What am I going to do? I can't let Dr Maaboottee leave. Winnie's going to give birth. But what am I going to say? Winnie's not due for weeks. How on earth can I explain that I know what's going to happen without mentioning the Mirrors of the Future Room? And then what? I might lose my job!

Panic exploded in Vincent's chest. Adrenaline surged through his body. A weird metallic taste leaked into his mouth.

Think, Vincent, THINK!

But Vincent couldn't think at all!

Whatever happens, right now I have to stop Dr Maaboottee leaving!

Vincent hurried over to Zelda and Dr Maaboottee. He had no idea what he was going to say let alone do.

'Zelda, Dr Maaboottee, Florence told me it's your wedding anniversary today. Happy anniversary!'

'Thank you, Vincent, thank you!' said Dr Maaboottee. 'Today I've been married to my African Queen for fifty years!'

'Yes, yes. Your African Queen . . .' *Think, Vincent, think!* 'Arh . . . um . . . Florence tells me you're off to celebrate.'

'That's right. Florence has organised a special surprise for us,' said Zelda.

'I'm sure it's something wonderful. Please, as a present from me, would you let me polish your shoes before you go? It would be my gift to both of you.'

'That's a lovely offer, Vincent, but I don't think we've got time,' said Zelda. 'Florence said our balloon is about to leave. There's two llamas waiting out the front now.' The Maaboottees never travelled by jet pack. Anywhere.

'Please,' pleaded Vincent. 'It won't take long. I promise!'

Zelda and Dr Maaboottee looked at Vincent and then each other. They could see how much it meant to him.

'Well, all right,' said Dr Maaboottee, 'but you'll have to be quick! We don't want to miss our balloon.'

'Of course not. I'll be quick.'

Vincent led Zelda and Dr Maaboottee over to his chair.

'Ladies first,' said Vincent. Zelda put her blue shoes on the shoe mounts. 'Ah, that's powder-blue with a touch of indigo and a bit of lapis lazuli if I'm not mistaken.'

Vincent began pulling stuff out of his drawers and wildly mixing polishes as if he was an artist or some mad scientist. 'They'll need a bit of this, with a touch of that and just a smidge of this . . . Hmmm, not quite, perhaps if I add a pinhead of black. Oh yes, that's getting closer.'

Vincent stretched out the mixing process as long as he could.

Dr Maaboottee looked at his watch.

'Got it! Perfect!' Vincent selected a brush and began painstakingly applying the meticulously matched polish to Zelda's shoes. Then he buffed and polished and buffed and polished till they shined like new.

'There,' he declared.

Zelda looked down at her shoes. 'Well, I never, Vincent. You are extraordinary! My shoes look as good as the first time I put them on in the shop. That's fifty years ago! Oh thank you, Vincent, they're my favourite shoes. I wore them at our wedding. Look at my shoes, dear.'

Dr Maaboottee looked down at his wife's shoes. 'Oh my, Vincent, you have done a *wonderful* job.'

Both Zelda and Dr Maaboottee looked as if they were about to cry.

It was Dr Maaboottee's turn. He got into the chair. Despite being dressed in his best suit, Dr Maaboottee was wearing the same boots he wore every other day. They were good strong, workboots but more than a little scuffed and dusty.

'Oh my, Vincent, lucky you got a hold of us before we left. Look at my boots. They're a sight.'

'Don't worry, Dr Maaboottee,' said Vincent, plucking bits of baobab bark from the doctor's socks. 'I know *just* what these boots need to make them look as good as new.'

Vincent dived into his shoe-cleaning kit and dug around. He pulled out a tube of this and a pot of that and began making up a mixture. Then he got out a small rag and began rubbing the mixture onto Dr Maaboottee's boots. And while he did, Vincent began telling the Maaboottees all about his grandfather and the story of his magic shoe-cleaning kit and how it had brought him here to The Grandest Hotel on Earth. Zelda and Dr Maaboottee were captivated. They completely lost track of time. It was only when Vincent – knowing full well it was too late in the morning for any balloon to take off – declared he was done, did they notice the time.

'Oh no,' gasped Zelda, covering her mouth with her hands, 'I think we've missed our balloon.'

Dr Maaboottee looked at his watch. It was almost eleven. By now it would be far too windy for any balloon to take off safely. 'Oh, my dear wife. You're right!'

'I feel *dreadful*,' cried Zelda. 'Florence will be so disappointed. She's gone to so much trouble to arrange a special surprise for us. She's been talking about it for weeks.'

Vincent put his head down and busied himself with his polishes, trying not to look at either of them.

Just as Dr Maaboottee was pulling on his boots, Florence came racing round the corner.

'ZELDA! DR MAABOOTTEE! Thank *goodness* you're still here. Winnie's gone into labour!'

Dr Maaboottee leapt out of the chair as fast as a man of his age could do such a thing and ran towards the Elephant House. Zelda ran after him.

'Come on,' cried Florence, tearing off. 'You don't want to miss this, Vincent!'

Vincent flung his 'Out to lunch' sign across his chair and took off after them.

Vincent thought watching an elephant being

born was surely one of the grandest things he would ever have the good fortune to witness. Winnie calmly bent her back legs and crouched so her baby didn't have far to fall as it entered this world in a gush. Then she gently nudged her newborn calf, who in a bag of blood and goo, lay still on the floor.

'He's not moving,' cried Florence. 'Is he all right, Dr Maaboottee?'

Standing off to the side, Dr Maaboottee looked concerned, but he didn't move. Instead he just watched. He understood that no one knew better than Winnie what needed to be done.

Winnie wrapped her trunk around her baby's trunk and gave it a pull. The calf slid a short distance across the wet floor.

Vincent and Florence gasped.

'Don't worry, Winnie knows what she's doing,' assured Dr Maaboottee.

But still the calf didn't move.

Winnie softly kicked it with her foot. She tugged it by the trunk again, lifting its head off the floor a little then letting it go.

Vincent and Florence gasped again as the newborn elephant's head hit the floor with a squelching *thwack*.

And then something happened. The calf lifted its right shoulder.

'He's moving!' cried Florence. 'He's alive!'

Winnie unwrapped her calf from the bag of goo. She nudged him up and onto his wobbly little legs.

But Dr Maaboottee still looked worried. 'He's up, Florry. But he's too small. He's not going to be able to drink his mother's milk.'

Dr Maaboottee was right. The calf had been born too soon. No matter how hard he tried, he wasn't tall enough to reach his mother's teat.

Winnie let out a distressed roar.

'Oh no!' cried Florence, who had a soft spot for The Grand's elephants the size of an elephant itself. She clicked the heels of her boots together nervously.

Vincent reached across and held her hand.

'It's all right, Winnie, it's all right,' reassured Dr Maaboottee, stroking Winnie's face. 'I can make up some milk that will be safe for your boy to drink.'

Winnie let out another distressed roar.

'Oh hurry, Dr Maaboottee, hurry,' cried Florence. 'I can't stand seeing Winnie so upset.'

Dr Maaboottee headed off to make up a bottle of milk. When he returned, Winnie let him approach her calf and before long he was drinking milk from the bottle. Winnie seemed to know instinctively her baby was now out of danger. She flapped her ears and let out a contented trumpet sound. While Dr Maaboottee held the bottle, Winnie kept touching her baby with her trunk and nudging him with her legs.

'She's letting him know everything's all right,' said Zelda. 'That Dr Maaboottee is a friend.'

'Thank goodness you hadn't left yet,' said Florence, taking off her glasses to wipe away a tear. 'I don't know *what* I would have done if she gave birth and you two weren't here. She wouldn't have let anyone else near her baby but you, Dr Maaboottee.'

Dr Maaboottee agreed. 'Yes, it could have turned out badly, but we had the luck of The Grand on our side today.'

Zelda laughed. 'We got so caught up getting our shoes polished and listening to Vincent's wonderful story about his grandfather we missed our balloon!'

'Looks like I might have to give them another polish,' said Vincent, looking at Dr Maaboottee's freshly polished boots, now covered in blood and goo.

'And while you do, perhaps you can come up with a name for him.' Dr Maaboottee nodded towards the baby elephant. 'After all if it wasn't for you, he might not be here.'

'You mean I get to name him?' said Vincent. His smiling eyes lit up the whole Elephant House.

'Oh, what a good idea!' said Florence. 'What are you going to call him?'

Vincent looked at the tiny baby elephant. 'What about Tommy? As in Tom Thumb because he's so small. And it's my little brother's name too.'

'Perfect!' cried Florence.

'Tommy it is then,' said Dr Maaboottee.

After the incredible event, Florence arranged for Dr Maaboottee and Zelda's anniversary picnic and the choir to be flown back from the next valley and brought to the Elephant House. There was no way Dr Maaboottee was going anywhere. Tommy would need almost ten litres of milk a day. Dr Maaboottee would have to feed him around the clock, just like a new mum.

'Here's to Tommy!' toasted Florence with a smoking soda. 'Welcome to The Grand!'

'To Tommy!' everyone cheered.

'And Vincent!' cried Florence.

'To Vincent!'

Vincent could feel himself blush. *If only they knew.*

CHAPTER 14

UNOPENED GIFTS AND THE SHORTEST STAIRCASE IN TOWN

'Elephant,' said Vincent, pointing at the picture. 'Today an elephant was born at the hotel and it's named after you, Thom. An elephant called Tommy. Just like you! What do you think about THAT?'

Thom took the picture and without looking at it dropped it on the kitchen floor and walked off.

'Not a lot,' said Rose. 'You should have named it after me.' She got up and began dancing the flamenco around the table as if that somehow proved her point.

Tap. Tap. Tap. STAMP! Tap. Tap. Tap. STAMP! Tap. Tap. Tap. STAMP!

'It was a boy!' pointed out Vincent.

Tap. Tap. Tap. STAMP! Tap. Tap. Tap. STAMP!

'What about Rosendo then?' *Tap. Tap. Tap. STAMP!* She flicked her cape in front of Vincent's face.

'Do you have to do that right now? Anyway, I thought you were Marilyn.'

Tap. Tap. Tap. STAMP! 'I am.'

Vincent shook his head and rolled his eyes.

'But when animals or streets are named after me, people can use my stage name or my real name, I don't mind.' *Tap. Tap. Tap. STAMP! Tap. Tap. Tap. STAMP! Tap. Tap. Tap. STAMP!*

'Well, that's useful to know.'

'Anyway, I don't think Thom even knows his name is Thom.'

'Of course he does!' said Vincent, defensively.

'If you say so.' Rose tapped and stamped off to her bedroom.

Vincent picked up his picture off the floor. He felt extra annoyed because he thought Rose was probably right. He wasn't sure Thom did know his own name. He remembered the time his mum had asked him to mind his brother for two minutes so she could dash to the shops and get some eardrops for

Rose. She'd barely been gone three seconds before Thom ran out the front gate and down the street. Vincent ran after him yelling, 'Thom, Thom, come back, Thom!' And never once did he turn around. As if he couldn't hear Vincent's panicked cries. As if it had never crossed his mind that his big brother would be chasing after him, trying to keep him safe. As if he didn't know his own name.

Vincent stared at the picture. He wished he could make his brother understand his elephant story more than anything. He so wanted Thom to know he'd saved a baby elephant and named it after him. *How many people have an elephant named after them? And it's not like it's going to happen again.* Vincent felt like he had the most amazing gift for Thom, but he couldn't give it to him.

Lying in bed that night, Vincent listened to Thom's screeching cries being extinguished by the soothing strains of Erik Satie's Gymnopédie No.1. It was one of Thom's favourites. Vincent's too. It was sad and soothing all at the same time. Vincent thought the music sounded like how his mum and dad must feel. All the gifts they couldn't give Thom. All the things they couldn't teach him. All the stories they couldn't share. All the hopes and dreams they'd had to let go. And the darkness and not knowing that took their place.

Vincent steered his mind back to the extraordinary events of the day. If he hadn't looked in the Mirrors of the Future Room, Winnie's baby might have died. Despite what Zelda said, nothing bad had happened. In fact, quite the opposite. He'd *stopped* bad things from happening. He'd helped save a baby elephant's life! THAT was a good thing. In fact THAT was incredible. And for the very first time Vincent felt like a bit of a hero.

Now all you modern readers have probably guessed that after the baby elephant incident, Vincent would return to the Mirrors of the Future Room.

And you'd be right.

However he didn't return once.

He returned several times.

In fact Vincent made a visit to the Mirrors of the Future Room a regular habit. And to make sure Zelda didn't become suspicious, he started getting out on the fifteenth floor and taking the fire stairs the rest of the way. Although he wasn't lying to

Zelda, he might as well have been. That was the bad thing about not being entirely honest. It usually involved a web of seemingly insignificant untruths and things you just conveniently forget to mention. And Vincent felt bad about that.

But not bad enough to stop doing it.

Vincent even began to wonder if he himself was becoming grand, like the Wainwright-Cunninghams. Surely another word for a grand person might be hero? So why would he stop now? Why should he?

Each time Vincent visited the Mirrors of the Future Room he experienced the same thing. First his brain felt like it was blowing a fuse. Then his scalp and hair tightened and burned as if they were on fire. And then the flash of blue-white lightning followed by a cryptic vision.

Although the meaning of the vision was never clear immediately, Vincent began to trust in time it would be. And when it was, suddenly everything slotted into place and Vincent would have to spring into action all at once. Like the second time Vincent went back to the room he saw a falling ladder and a tree bent over so far its leaves swept the ground like a broom. A week later when Vincent was having lunch in the treetops with Florence and the sloths, Florence mentioned to Fin that he needed to be careful because a howling wind was forecast for the afternoon. Vincent knew then and there that *that* wind was going to blow a ladder down. But which ladder?

Straightaway Vincent excused himself from lunch, slid down the tree, pedalled the swan boat back across the lake and walked right round the whole hotel until he spotted a lone window cleaner high up on a ladder. He was scrubbing giraffe slobber off the breakfast-room windows. *I can't just stand here and hold the ladder till the wind comes,* thought Vincent. So he ran as fast as he could back around the hotel and up to the breakfast room. Then he casually wandered over to the window and started chatting to the window cleaner about giraffe slobber and what messy eaters they were and an idea he had to make his shoes safer. Just when Vincent had completely run out of things to talk about, a huge gust of wind came out of nowhere. It lifted the ladder and blew it up and away from the wall. The window cleaner screamed and Vincent grabbed him by the arm, a microsecond before the ladder fell and crashed to the ground. Vincent held on to the cleaner – who was a solid fellow – until he thought his arm was going to rip right out of its socket, at which time Rupert arrived to help haul the cleaner inside to safety.

The next time Vincent visited the room he saw a crying baby and a pile of dirty sheets. A few days later a guest came running through the lobby screaming, 'I've lost my baby! Please! Someone help me! I CAN'T FIND MY BABY!'

Rupert managed to get a description of the baby from its now hysterical mother and then grabbed his megaphone. 'Attention, all staff. Stop what you're doing. This is a rrr-red alert. I rrr-repeat . . .' (Even in an emergency Rupert rolled his 'R's.) 'This is a rrr-red alert. Stop what you are doing immediately and look for a baby last seen sucking a large blue dummy and wearing a penguin onesie.' Vincent was about to join the search party when he realised he knew exactly where the baby was.

What am I going to do? I can't find the baby. It'll look too suspicious. But I can't just leave it there.

The lobby cleaners Luz and Tracee flew past. 'Here, bubba. Come to Luz and Tracee, bubba.'

'Where are you going?' asked Vincent.

'Chocolate Lounge. Even baby can smell double fudge banana balls.'

'He's not there, I've already looked. You guys check the laundry. I'll check the library.'

Luz and Tracee made a U-turn and hightailed it off to the laundry. When they re-emerged with the infant in their arms, the celebration was – as you might expect – grand. A lost then found infant is a source of out-of-body terror and torrential relief – for *everyone*. And always requires the grandest of celebrations. That night nearly every guest joined in at the Transatlantic Ballroom. Luz and Tracee were the queens of the night and watching hundreds of folks dancing the 'throw them bones' was a sight to make the heaviest heart fly. Once the baby's mother recovered, she danced with that penguin baby till she could dance no more. And the story of the baby that had crawled into a laundry chute and shot down four storeys only to land safely in a pile of dirty sheets would go on to become a favourite tale at The Grand, a hotel so full of stories you could sit in front of a fire telling them for a year without ever drawing breath or repeating a single one.

Once again Vincent felt like he had done something incredible. He'd saved not only a baby elephant but a human baby too. And when Vincent herded all the animals from the lowest part of the valley to the top of the mountain, saving them from a flash flood and stopped a batch of off seafood being served to a full dining room he began to think he knew better than Florence or her grandmother about leaving some things up to the gods. As far as Vincent was concerned, knowing what was going to happen at The Grand was a *necessity* and if no one else was brave enough to do it, then it was going to have to be him. (Don't you love how brains do that? Hide our real motives under a chair and then dazzle us with explanations that sound so good they must be true!) *Not* going into the Mirrors of the Future Room was never anything to do with bravery. Yes, Vincent had saved animals and people. Yes, he'd stopped bad things from happening. But did that make what he was doing right? Was he really in control of the future?

My co-author just pointed out that the staircase from 'being humble and having healthy doubts about yourself' to 'thinking you're pretty special' can be a very short one.

And Vincent was about to learn that the hard way.

CHAPTER 15

TOMATO SANDWICHES ON THE PLATFORM FOR THE RECKLESS

Singing rapper MZee's latest song, Vincent skipped up the fire stairs to the sixteenth floor. He'd climbed them so many times he no longer bothered to be quiet or in any way discreet. He kicked the door wide open with his boot and headed straight down the corridor to the Mirrors of the Future Room, a swagger in his step.

Every time Vincent visited the room, without noticing he was doing it, he opened the door the smallest fraction wider than the time before. But this time, he was so relaxed he turned the doorknob without so much as a thought. The lock bolt popped straight out, practically sucking the door – and Vincent with it – right into the room. Vincent stumbled forward. For the first time, he saw his own face in the mirror. Vincent wrenched the door back towards himself.

But it was too late.

A bolt of energy travelled up his spine pummelling him like a freight train.

His body arched.

His head flew backwards.

The inside of his brain felt like an exploding star. His scalp and hair blown to smithereens.

Vincent gripped the doorhandle, trying to stay upright as the bolt of blue-white lightning struck.

And then the vision. Violent and rapid-fire like a machine gun straight into his brain.

Florence lying in a hospital bed attached to machines.

His mum and dad hugging him, the three of them laughing together in a happy embrace.

Vincent looks down at his feet and sees Florence's emerald boots.

Vincent flew backwards. His head hit the floor as the door slammed shut.

At that moment in time, somewhere deep inside, Vincent understood everything.

He got up and charged towards the fire stairs. He flew down them as fast as he could, jumping three at a time, stumbling, getting up then stumbling again. He wished he could outrun himself. He wished he could run back through time. He wished he could undo what he had done. And more than anything, Vincent wished he could unsee what he had just seen.

Standing in the stairwell, hands on his knees, Vincent tried to slow his breathing. Sweat dripped from his forehead. He watched it splash silently onto the stairs – *drip, drip, drip* – his heart thumping in his ears as if his head was inside a wooden drum. Vincent's hands and feet went numb as a feeling of panic tightened around his body like a snake. *Get a grip, Vincent. Get A GRIP!*

It took a while for Vincent to compose himself. When the elevator doors opened, Zelda looked up and smiled, same as she always did.

'Weren't you supposed to collect a pair of shoes?' she asked.

'What?' replied Vincent. He was so completely rattled he'd forgotten the little insignificant lie he'd told Zelda on the way up. 'Oh, yes . . . yes . . .' He swallowed. 'They . . . they must have forgotten. I looked everywhere. Couldn't find any shoes.'

'Never mind,' said Zelda, brightly. 'One less pair to polish!'

Vincent nodded and stared at the floor. He touched his hair nervously, checking it was still there. He was too scared to even look at Zelda. Surely she'd be able to see right through him.

Vincent got out at the lobby and walked over to his chair. He pulled Min out of his pocket and held her up to his cheek

What had just happened? What had he done?

Vincent knew the visions were connected, just like all the other visions had been. And while the future looked great for him, the future for Florence looked frightening. How could his happiness be connected to something terrible happening to her? It didn't make sense. How could that be? And why? Why? Why would this be?

Vincent's whole body filled up with deep regret. And fear. A fear so bad it made him want to scream. A fear so bad it made him want to run and run and never stop.

'Hey, Vincent. What's up?'

Emerald boots. It was Florence. He looked up into her kind, beautiful eyes.

'What's wrong?' asked Florence. 'You look like you've seen a ghost!'

'Do I? No, I'm fine,' said Vincent, scrambling to look and sound normal, as if he hadn't just seen the most terrible future imaginable for Florence.

'You sure? You look a bit pale.'

'Well, I do have a bit of a headache actually.' (Which was the truth.) 'Sometimes I breathe in too much polish. I think I just need some fresh air.' While he was saying one thing, inside his head Vincent was screaming. *What's going to happen to you? Whatever's going to happen to you?*

'Well, how about lunch on the platform then? Plenty of fresh air up there.'

Vincent nodded.

'Great! See you in fifteen.'

Vincent watched Florence as she skipped across the lobby. Her cinnamon hair swished from side to side. Her emerald boots playing Bach's Cello Suite No. 1 in G Major. Along the way she stopped to fix a pony's headdress, hug a guest's baby, applaud a wandering minstrel and talk to the herpetologist who was polishing the turtles. Vincent's head throbbed and his heart stung. Being friends with Florence was the best. She was generous and kind and worldly and smart and capable and funny. Why hadn't he listened to her? Why had he done what he'd done? And why did she have to get sick? What if it was worse? What if Florence . . . Vincent shut the thought down. He couldn't bear to even think it.

Florence couldn't not be around.

She just couldn't!

Surely without her there would be no Grand! As far as Vincent was concerned, Florence *was* The Grand!

But why was he wearing her boots in the vision?

How could his happiness and Florence getting sick coexist, let alone be connected? It just wasn't possible.

Vincent caught the chairlift up to the platform. He watched as an old lady wearing a winged suit jumped off and flew down over the valley while Florence, legs dangling, kept an eye on her through her binoculars.

'I hope I'm that fearless when I'm old,' said Florence. She tossed Vincent a brown bag. 'And I hope tomato sandwiches are all right.'

Vincent sat down next to her and unwrapped his sandwich. 'You've converted me.'

His head still throbbed where it had smacked against the floor. Everything in his body felt like it was going too fast. His heart. His blood. His brain.

'Oh, look! An eagle,' cried Florence. She dropped her half-eaten sandwich into her lap and grabbed her binoculars again.

'Where?'

'Over there,' she said, pointing, 'above the tree house.'

'Oh, I see him. I think it's a condor.'

'It is too. It's an Andean condor. Look at its wings! They must be ten feet across.'

'I hope there's no small kids in the tree house,' worried Vincent. 'He's big enough to take one.'

'Don't worry, a wildlife ranger will be close by. They'll be keeping an eye on things.'

Florence and Vincent ate their tomato sand-wiches and watched the condor glide in circles as it rode the thermals down, then up, then down again. But Vincent wasn't really watching. All he could see was the vision of Florence lying in a hospital bed. He wanted to tell her so badly. She was as wise as an owl. She'd know what to do.

But he couldn't do that.

Knowing something really bad was going to happen was a terrible, terrible thing. Already Vincent's whole body was bracing itself. Like that terrifying freefall feeling when you miss a step.

Florence lay back on the platform and looked up at the sky. 'Do you know, I never even took a lunch break before you started working here.'

Vincent lay back too.

'I always told myself I had too much to do – which I did! And I still have too much to do, but I think it was because there was never anyone to have lunch with. I mean, there's Rupert and Zelda and Dr Maaboottee and everyone, but they're more like aunties and uncles. It's not the same as having a friend my own age. I mean, you know who MZee is. And you don't mind getting thrashed on a rocking horse.'

'I do mind getting thrashed on a rocking horse,' protested Vincent, weakly.

Florence laughed.

She had the best laugh.

'This has been such a fun summer. It's made me realise how much I've missed having a friend to talk to and do stuff with. You know, regular kid stuff. And you understand my work too. Most kids don't have to work like we do.'

'I don't think you can compare my work to yours. What you do matters. I just shine shoes.'

'You do a lot more than just shine shoes, Vincent.' Florence reached across and grabbed his hand. She squeezed it tight. As they lay there staring up at the sky, Vincent knew Florence was the sort of friend he might be lucky enough to find *once* in his life but *never* twice.

While in the past he'd accepted the future in the visions was going to happen, this time he couldn't.

This time he had to STOP it happening.

Somehow, someway, he had to stop the future before it arrived if it was the very last thing he did.

And while he couldn't say it out loud, lying there Vincent solemnly committed every bone, every muscle and every cell in his body to the protection of Florence.

'I better get back to work,' said Florence, hopping up. 'The llamas are getting shampooed this arvo, the Fizzy Room's not fizzy for some reason and we're completely out of whatever-flavour-you-think-of balls. You have no idea how many thousands of those things we go through in a week, Vincent. It's impossible to keep up.'

Vincent scrambled to his feet. 'Hey, careful! Don't stand so close to the edge.'

'Don't be a worrywart. Come on, I'll race you.' Florence turned, jumped off the platform and ran down the mountain.

Vincent ran after her. 'Watch out, Florence!' he yelled, leaping over rocks and hollows. 'You'll fall!'

CHAPTER 16

STOPPING THE FUTURE

From that moment on, Vincent approached every day as a mission to keep Florence safe from harm. He had no idea how or even what he needed to protect Florence from. That was the hardest part. How do you prepare if you don't know who or what someone needs protection from? Or even where! Would he need brains or strength? Cunning or intuition? Did he need to be her sword or shield? Vincent reassured himself he just needed to be vigilant and ready at *all* times. He'd managed every other time to know when the future was about to happen. And he hoped with all his heart this time would be the same.

Luckily for Vincent, Florence spent a lot of time at the front desk where he could keep an eye on her. But every time she walked off, Vincent stopped what he was doing and followed her. He followed her to the Grand Theatre to meet the new director who'd flown in from New York. He followed her to a meeting with the lepidopterists, who were preparing for the arrival of three new species of butterfly. He followed her to Tenzing, the rotating mountaintop restaurant where window cleaners were carrying out the dangerous job of de-icing the glass roof. And he followed her to the doughnut bar to sample the latest flavour – the hot-fizzing-double-dipped-treacle-cream kaboom.

But a few days later, with the vision as clear as a picture book in his mind, Florence walked past Vincent's chair on her way to the elevator.

'Morning, Vincent!' she said, bright and breezy. 'Hot springs or sloths for lunch?'

'Hmmm, sloths?' he replied, trying to sound just as bright and breezy.

As soon as the elevator doors closed, Vincent rushed over. He watched the light flick from 'L' to 'GF' and down to 'B'.

The basement.

Florence was getting out in the basement. Vincent took the fire stairs and ran down as fast as he could. When he opened the basement door he heard a loud beeping sound. *BEEP BEEP BEEP*. A huge truck, rear lights flashing, was backing into the loading bay. And Florence was standing right behind it!

'Keep coming . . .' she yelled, waving at the driver. 'You've got plenty of room.'

Vincent panicked. He sprinted towards Florence. But before he reached her, Florence had stepped out of the way and the truck reversed safely into the loading bay. Vincent ducked behind a pylon. A man got out of the truck and walked over to Florence.

'Here you go, love.' He handed her a clipboard.

'Oh, goody, the new bedspreads from Kashmir. I can't wait to see them.'

Two more men got out, opened the back doors and pulled down a ramp. Then they picked up a huge wide container and tried to manoeuvre it out of the truck.

'Dip the left front side down a bit and swing the right back up,' said Florence.

But the men struggled.

'Watch out!'

'Grab it underneath!'

'I am!' yelled the man on the ramp to the man inside the truck. 'It's heavy!'

'Try tipping it to the left.'

'I can't, my hands are slipping!'

Florence was standing at the bottom of the ramp as the man, his face as red and shiny as a ripe cherry, began to slide backwards.

Vincent didn't wait around to see which way the huge container was going to fall. He leapt out from behind the pylon and dived at Florence, knocking her out of the way. Florence slammed onto the concrete floor, Vincent on top of her. Her glasses flew across the ground. Min yelped. So did Emerson.

'Vincent!' she yelled. 'What did you do that for?'

The men on the truck stood there, still holding the heavy container, the looks on all their faces asking Vincent the very same question.

'Sorry, Florence! I thought that container was about to fall on you.'

Florence stood up and dusted herself off. Vincent retrieved her glasses, which thankfully hadn't broken, but her knees were bleeding and the heel of her hand was grazed and red.

Both of them checked their pocket dogs. Min was shaking.

The men on the truck navigated the container safely down the ramp and onto the unloading dock.

'What are you doing here anyway, Vincent?'

'Um.' Vincent had to think quick. 'Um, my new polishes are meant to be delivered today. I thought I'd come down and see if they'd arrived. I've almost run out of mulberry purple and periwinkle blue. And I'm in desperate need of black and indigo and . . .' Vincent listed off a long catalogue of colours he'd supposedly run out of. He even made some up, remembering the bigger the lie, the more likely people were to believe it.

'Oh,' said Florence, 'I haven't heard anything about a polish delivery. I'll chase it up.'

'And maybe just stand a bit further away from the truck next time,' suggested Vincent. 'Just in case.'

Florence looked annoyed. 'I've supervised the loading and unloading of thousands of trucks, Vincent. Don't forget I've lived at The Grand my whole life. And I like to think I run the place pretty well. I don't want to sound rude, but it was you that mucked that up, not me!'

'True. But you were standing very close.'

'I know, you're just trying to protect me. So I

shouldn't really be angry. Next time, I'll stand back. Promise.'

'Good,' said Vincent, relieved.

'You know you don't need to worry about me,' said Florence, a quizzical look on her face. 'I do know what I'm doing.'

Another truck arrived and Florence went back to supervising deliveries. Vincent had no choice but to head up to the lobby. He only stopped worrying when Florence emerged from the elevator and went back to work behind the front desk where he could keep an eye on her.

Later that day, an old woman – not the one in the winged suit – arrived for a shoeshine.

'Oh, this is a comfy chair,' she said. 'I'd be happy to sit here all afternoon.'

Vincent examined her shoes. They were old and the soles were worn through. They also ponged, but he did his very best to pretend they didn't.

'Sorry. They're not very glamourous, dear,' she said, 'but they're comfortable. I have terrible corns you see. *Ooww*, they're so painful.'

While he polished and mended her shoes, the old lady told Vincent her life story. He loved hearing about his customers' lives. It was one of the fringe benefits of the job. 'I was a midwife for sixty years, you see. I've probably brought about twenty thousand babies into the world. The first baby I ever delivered is a grandmother now. Would you believe it?'

Vincent rummaged around in his box for the right shade of white. He also started thinking about llama wool and how he might use it to make some special patches to stop her corns rubbing.

'This is a treat,' said the old lady, relaxing back into the chair. 'Don't mind me if I nod off, will you?'

Just then Vincent saw Florence wander over to Luz and Tracee, who were mopping the lobby floor in their usual funky way. As they chatted Vincent's bones clicked into high alert. He looked up at the ceiling. Florence was standing right under the chandelier, the same one Max had used as a swing.

'That's it!' Suddenly in his mind Vincent saw chains snap. Moose antlers bouncing and splintering into twigs. Exploding light bulbs, scattering across the floor like diamonds. And Florence crushed, her two emerald boots sticking out beneath the fallen chandelier like the Wicked Witch of the East in *The Wizard of Oz*.

Vincent – still holding the old lady's shoe – bolted across the lobby to rescue her.

'FLORENCE!' he yelled, 'FLORENCE!'

Florence turned just in time to see Vincent slip and fall on the still-wet floor and come barrelling towards them like a bowling ball with a set of out-stretched arms. Just in time to *see* it, but not, I'm afraid, in time to do anything about it.

'Arghhhhhhhh!'

Vincent crashed into Luz, Tracee and Florence.

Strike! All three of them fell to the floor like bowling pins.

'Oow, my mabungo!' yelled Luz, rubbing her bottom while trying to untangle her limbs from the others. 'Vincent, why you do that? How am I going to dance the Milly Rock with a broken mabungo?'

'Oh, my knee!' cried Tracee. 'I can't do Crispy Duck with bung knee!'

Florence, remarkably unhurt, helped Luz and Tracee to their feet. She ordered wheel-chairs and cold packs and sent them both off to Dr Nelson at the hotel hospital. And, despite no broken bones, Florence insisted they take the rest of the week off.

'I'm so sorry, Florence,' said Vincent, unable

to explain at all why he'd been running across the lobby in the first place.

'Don't worry,' she said. 'Accidents happen. Even at The Grand.'

But Vincent could tell Florence was furious. Twice in one day? Who wouldn't be? No doubt what she really wanted to say was *Listen, Vincent, you do your job and leave me to do mine!* After all, running The Grand was hard enough without him making it harder.

Florence went back to her duties at the front desk. Vincent picked up the old lady's shoe and returned to his chair. But when he got there, the old lady was gone. *She must have hobbled off barefoot!* Vincent was horrified. He had been so distracted he hadn't even asked her name or what room she was in or anything. How was he going to return her shoe?

For the rest of the day, Vincent tried to bury his bad feelings by throwing himself into his work. By early evening, he'd managed to get through the pile of shoes that had stacked up and the disasters of the day began to fade. But Vincent was worried. How could he possibly keep this up? Protecting Florence from anything and everything was impossible. He was bruised from all the falls and completely frazzled from being on constant high alert. And then there was his own work. Vincent decided the answer was he didn't have a choice. He packed up for the day and headed home. He felt sure if he could get a good night's sleep he'd be better able to tackle things tomorrow.

CHAPTER 17

WEEK TWO OF CHANGING THE FUTURE

The next few weeks were more of the same. Every time Florence left the lobby, Vincent stopped what he was doing and shadowed her, ready to rescue her from anything and everything. But nothing bad happened. The only bad things that happened were Vincent's attempts to save Florence from the dangers he imagined.

Beside Vincent's chair, the pile of shoes grew, along with complaints from guests about the wrong colour polish, shoddy repairs or even worse, shoes that had gone missing altogether.

And each day Vincent's behaviour became more

and more erratic and the stories to explain himself more outrageous.

While Vincent was in a state of constant anxiety, waiting for the terrible event to occur, Florence became equally troubled. Vincent had gone from being her closest friend to someone she struggled to understand at all. When he started he was the best shoeshiner The Grand had ever had and now he was one of the worst. Florence began to dread seeing him. What was she going to do? It was her job to run The Grand the way The Grand was meant to be run. Vincent was not just messing up his job; he was messing up hers as well.

Florence's insomnia worsened. She lay awake, worrying into the small hours of the morning. At times like these she wished she had her mum or dad around. They'd know what to do. But they were trying to track down a wild ass in the Horn of Africa and had been out of phone range for weeks. Eventually, she consulted Dr Maaboottee.

'I wish I could help you, Florry, but elephants are my specialty, I'm afraid. Zelda and I never had children so I'm no expert at what goes on inside the brain of an eleven-year-old boy. And I'm too old to remember! But I will tell you this, that boy loves you like family. He would never mean to harm you or The Grand.'

Florence knew that was true. Which only made things worse.

'Why don't you just ask him what's going on?' suggested Dr Maaboottee.

So the next day, as they ate lunch on the Platform for the Reckless, Florence did.

'Is everything okay, Vincent?'

'Of course!' he answered through a fake smile. 'Why?'

'Come on, Vincent. You know and I know, your mind is not on the job like it used to be. I keep turning around and there you are. You're hardly ever at your chair.'

Vincent apologised. He made up stories about troubles he was having at home and difficult guests, et cetera et cetera. 'But I promise, Florence, I've got it under control now. You don't need to worry, I'm back on track. You'll see.'

Florence didn't know why but she felt strangely unconvinced.

'You can tell me anything, you know that, don't you, Vincent?'

'Of course I do. I'll never forget my first night at

The Grand and talking to you about Thom. You're the only person I can talk to about a lot of stuff, Florence. That's why you're such a good friend.'

'I feel the same way, Vincent. That's why I've been so worried. I'd feel dreadful if you had a problem you felt you couldn't talk to me about.'

After their conversation Vincent arrived early to work and left late. The pile of shoes shrank. The complaints stopped. But he couldn't keep it up. Within days, the pile was growing again and Vincent returned to causing havoc as he shadowed Florence everywhere like a bad dream.

Florence ordered Vincent to spend his lunch hour in the Let It Be Room in the hope it would take the edge off his jittery self, which saw disaster everywhere. When that didn't work she sent him to see Dr Nelson at the hotel hospital, thinking he must be suffering some sort of catastrophising disorder. But no matter how much Florence protested that she knew what she was doing, that she'd been running the hotel – successfully and safely – for years, Vincent kept insisting that she needed to beware. That the sloths could well become aggressive and shred her to pieces. (My co-author is in stitches!) Or that it wasn't far-fetched to suggest baby turtles might be related closely enough to piranhas to eat her alive and she simply mustn't put her hand in the fountain again.

Eventually, Florence was at her wits' end. She called Rupert into the front office. She closed the door and burst into tears. Running a huge hotel was a lot for an eleven-year-old girl, even one as grand as Florence.

'Oh, Rupert, I don't know what to do! I've tried everything, but Vincent keeps messing up. Have you seen the pile of shoes?' Rupert nodded sympathisingly. 'And I can barely keep up with the complaints.'

Florence covered her mouth with her hand, a last-ditch attempt not to utter the words she was about to say.

'I can't keep Vincent as our shoeshine boy any longer, but I can't bear the thought of him not being here. He's my best friend. How can I ask my best friend to leave? But I can't do my job with him leaping out from behind chairs and trees and tackling me.'

Rupert handed Florence a tissue and wrapped her up in a big hug.

'Oh, Florry, I know,' he said. 'I know how hard this is for you. I love Vincent too. He's such a lovely boy. And so talented with shoes! He rrr-really is the best shoeshiner we've ever had. Well, he was.

I've no idea what's going on with him, Florry.' The ends of Rupert's moustache rotated, a bit like a satellite dish following the night sky.

Rupert put his hands on Florence's shoulders and looked her straight in the eye. 'But you know as well as I do, Florry, we have a job to do. *We* are The Grandest Hotel on Earth! And it's our job to make sure as many people as possible get a bit of grand. At the end of the day, *nothing's* more important than that.'

Florence understood what Rupert was saying. She'd run out of options.

'But Vincent loves The Grand as much as we do. He'll be devastated,' she sobbed. Florence's glasses steamed up. Tears fell from her golf-ball cheeks and rolled off her feathered collar.

'I know. It's not easy being grand, but you're doing a sterling job, Florry.'

She nodded. 'I'll tell him this afternoon.'

Rupert wiped away a tear from his own eye. 'You're doing the rrr-right thing, Florry.'

She gave him a hug. 'Thanks, Rupert.'

Florence opened the office door to leave, but as she did a great weight pushed against it, sending it flying into the room and straight into her face.

'Ooww!' she cried. She reached up and cupped her nose. It was bleeding.

She looked down. There, lying on the floor, was Vincent.

'Vincent! What are you doing?'

Rupert grabbed a tissue and sat her back down in the chair. 'Tilt your head back, Florry, to stop the bleeding.'

Vincent picked himself up.

'I'm so sorry, Florence. You don't need to say anything. I heard everything. I didn't mean to eavesdrop. Please don't feel bad. This is all my fault. I'm so sorry for messing things up.'

Florence started crying again.

Vincent wanted more than anything to explain his behaviour to her. But if he couldn't save Florence from the terrible future, at least he could save her from the crushing, unbearable burden of knowing what was to come. The dread he carried day in, day out. The feeling that the whole world was made of glass and his shoes were lead. Every atom of his being ached with tension, his entire body hummed with fear. He couldn't do that to Florence! He would carry the fear *for* her. He had to.

'Please don't cry, Florence. Please.'

'I can't help it.' Tears streamed down her face. 'I'm so sorry, Vincent.'

'You don't need to be. Working at The Grand has been the best thing that has ever happened to me. Ever.'

'I know. And that makes it so much worse,' she sobbed. 'I hope we'll still be friends.'

'Of course. Nothing will ever change that, Florence. Nothing.' And they hugged each other tight.

'Oh, I hope so, Vincent. Promise you'll come back and visit me? And see baby Tommy? You could bring Thom. And Rose. The whole family.'

'I promise,' reassured Vincent.

'You're my best friend forever, Vincent, no matter what.'

'Same,' said Vincent, 'same.'

Vincent went back to his chair to pack up his things.

Florence sat in the office and cried while Rupert rubbed her back. She hated the idea of running The Grandest Hotel on Earth alone again, without Vincent. But what choice did she have?

Before packing up, Vincent polished and repaired every pair of waiting shoes. Then he collected up all his pots of polish, all his brushes and rags, all his special inserts and potions and sprays. He took Min out of his pocket and sat her on his empty red chair. He took off his uniform and hung it up on the hook. He loved his grand uniform. It was the most beautiful piece of clothing he'd ever worn. How he would miss it. And how he would miss his green neon shoeshine sign and his grand leather chair.

Vincent picked up Min and walked around the lobby one last time. He watched the dog-sized ponies with their feathered headdresses delivering nibbles and drinks never spilling a drop. He marvelled at the epic view of snow-capped peaks and the tiny finches that swooped and flitted across the room. As the double bass players plucked their strings, it began to sink in just how much he was going to miss The Grandest Hotel on Earth.

Everyone gathered to say their goodbyes.

'For you, Vincent,' said Luz. She handed him a full set of instructional dance step postcards. 'You good with shoes but possibly worst dancer we ever see. Practice, practice. And remember, for a bit of grand feeling, do "living my best life".' Luz held out her hands as if she was holding two plates up high, shook her shoulders up and down like pistons and slid her feet from side to side. 'Work every time.'

189

'I will,' he promised. He gave Luz and Tracee a hug.

Next it was time to say goodbye to Rupert. He engulfed Vincent in a bear hug. 'Now Min is far too attached to you to be left behind, you take her with you, you hear? Once outside the hotel grounds she'll grow twenty times in size, but she'll be just as loveable.'

Vincent could hear Rupert's voice crumble. He really was going to miss Vincent and Vincent was really going to miss him.

'I wish I could but I can't. Thom's just not good with animals.' Vincent's voice crumbled too. He kissed Min and handed her to Rupert.

'Don't worry, Waldo loves company.' Rupert's pocket dog, Waldo, and Min rumbled as they worked out their squishy new pocket arrangement.

Vincent's eyes stung with tears. The idea of not seeing Min every day felt like someone had punctured his heart and all the blood in his body was falling to his feet.

'You'll come back and see Tommy, won't you, Vincent?' said Dr Maaboottee, ruffling his hair. 'And I can always use a spare pair of hands at the Elephant House.'

'I will, Dr Maaboottee. And if you have any problems matching the colour of those sandals, Zelda, just bring them down to Barry. I'll fix them for you.'

'You will? Come here, Vincent, and let me give you a squeeze.' Zelda gave Vincent a big hug. An ocean of feelings rose up inside him. The sadness he felt that his grandfather was gone, about leaving Min and no longer being the shoeshine boy at The Grandest Hotel on Earth. All his worries about Thom and his family. And worst of all the fears he had for Florence and the terrible vision of what was to come.

Vincent didn't want to, but he couldn't hold it back anymore. He began to cry. How he wished he could explain to everyone why he'd been behaving like a complete idiot. He wanted to tell them what he'd seen and to watch out for Florence. But while that might have made him feel better, he knew it wouldn't help them.

'It's going to be okay, Vincent,' reassured Zelda, squeezing him tight. 'I can feel it in my bones. I know you're going to miss The Grand and, boy, is The Grand going to miss you. But good things always come from bad. You never know what the future has in store.'

Yes, I do! Vincent felt like screaming: *YES, I DO!*

As Vincent walked down the driveway with his beaten-up old shoe-cleaning kit in one hand and his wooden stool in the other, he didn't even realise he'd left the road until he found himself in the Junkyard of Broken and Abandoned Dreams. Standing there, Vincent still couldn't believe his time at The Grandest Hotel on Earth had really and truly come to an end. While he'd never understood what a Junkyard of Broken and Abandoned Dreams could possibly have to do with grand, he did now. He walked around and started picking up stones and bits of deadwood and yellow dandelions. Then he knelt down, cleared a patch of long grass and built a small shrine. He found the emerald polish he'd used to clean Florence's boots and balanced it carefully on the top. Although he didn't really know how, he closed his eyes and tried as hard as he could to let go of his dream to save Florence from the bad thing in her future.

Not because he didn't want to save her, but because he knew he couldn't.

And with that, Vincent rose to his feet and walked out the gates of The Grandest Hotel on Earth.

CHAPTER 18

HOME

Waking up and not going to The Grandest Hotel on Earth was possibly the worst feeling on earth. Vincent lay there, staring up at the curls of peeling paint that hung from the ceiling. Before working at The Grand, Vincent struggled to haul himself out of bed, but The Grand had changed everything. Each and every day he'd leapt out like a happy frog at the first pitter-patter of warm summer rain.

Suddenly he had somewhere to be!

Suddenly he had something he could do!

Suddenly he was someone!

He was the shoeshine boy at The Grandest Hotel on Earth!

But now he was just ordinary Vincent again. He felt like every scoop on his towering ice-cream cone had toppled over and fallen into a giant pile of elephant poop.

Rose stuck her head round the door. 'What's that word when you get what you deserve? Hang on, I remember. Karma! That's it. If you'd taken me with you, this would never have happened!'

'Go away, Rose.' Vincent rolled over and faced the wall. 'You have no idea what you're talking about. There's no such thing as karma. And I know that for a fact. Bad things happen to good people all the time. That's just the way it is.'

'Well, if it's not karma, maybe they realised how *ordinary* you are, Vincent. I don't know why they didn't pick me in the first place. I can do grand. I'm an actress after all!'

'I don't know, Rose,' replied Vincent, coolly, 'maybe it's because you're seven? Or maybe it's because you know NOTHING about shoes?' Vincent rolled over to face her. 'OR MAYBE IT'S BECAUSE YOU WALK AROUND EVERYWHERE WEARING A DISGUSTING OLD BLANKET!'

Rose's chin twitched and wobbled as she tried not to cry.

Vincent instantly regretted losing his temper. But he couldn't help it.

His mum walked into the bedroom. 'What's going on?'

'Nothing,' mumbled Vincent. He put a pillow over his face.

'Rose, leave your brother alone. For someone who's supposed to be an actress, you're not being very sensitive right now.'

'But that was my shot at the big time and HE BLEW IT!'

'That's enough, Rose! I said not now.'

'It wasn't YOUR shot at anything,' snapped Vincent.

'Will you two stop it! You know how yelling upsets your brother.'

'Oh yeah. That's right, I forgot,' snarled Rose. 'Thom's the only one who's allowed to scream in this house.'

'Rose!'

'MARILYN! Rose is that poor girl who has that weirdo for a brother. I'm Marilyn. I'm a movie star and I don't HAVE any brothers!' Rose twirled her cape and stomped off in her plastic fluffy high-heeled slippers.

Vincent understood how Rose felt. At home, everything was always about Thom. He'd forgotten just how crappy and invisible that could make you feel.

Vincent stayed in his bedroom for days.

He didn't speak unless spoken to.

He barely ate a thing.

And the same thoughts went round and round his head like a pop song. *I've mucked up. I've left Florence alone. I should have found a way to save her. Rose is right. I blew it. I blew everything.*

Each day, Vincent felt a little worse than the day before. It got so bad, even Rose tried to cheer him up. She came into his room, her tap shoes on and danced around his bed.

'This is a special dance, Vincent,' she announced, flapping her cape up and down like a bird. 'An ancient dance to mend your soul.'

Tap. Tap. Tap. STAMP! Tap. Tap. Tap. STAMP! Tap. Tap. Tap. STAMP!

Vincent couldn't tell the difference between this dance and all her other dances. But he appreciated the effort.

'Thanks,' he said. 'That actually made me feel a bit better.'

'That's good!' declared Rose, clearly delighted. 'Now's probably a good time to tell you I lost that scooter Dad found for you at council pick-up.'

'WHAT?'

'Don't blame me, I'm innocent!' screamed Rose, running from the room. 'I just left it in the park. Some thief stole it.'

'I'M GOING TO KILL YOU, ROSE!' yelled Vincent.

Vincent flew out of bed and chased Rose into the kitchen. His mum was at the stove, boiling eggs. Thom was lying on the floor like a sleeping snow angel as Erik Satie's Gymnopédie No.1 flowed around the room. Rose jumped over Thom and ran around the kitchen table, clearly enjoying the pursuit. Vincent ran after her.

'Vincent! Rose! Stop it, you two.'

'She lost my scooter!'

'Yeah, well, Thom tore up your postcards from The Grand!'

Vincent stopped chasing Rose. He looked at his mother. 'He didn't, did he?'

'Not all of them, Vincent. I saved a few. And we can sticky tape the others. I've got all the pieces,' she said, trying to console him. 'Don't be angry with him, Vincent. It's not his fault, he doesn't understand.'

But Vincent was angry. Wildly angry.

He walked over to Thom, who hadn't even realised he'd been used like a jump at a pony club gymkhana. Vincent snorted with fury. Then he kicked Thom in the leg. Thom wailed. Vincent looked as shocked as Thom did.

'VINCENT!' screamed his mother. 'How could you? You're his big brother. When will you start acting like one?'

'What's the point?' spat Vincent. 'He doesn't even know I'm his big brother!'

Vincent walked out the front door and slammed it shut. He ran down Standard Street. And he kept on running till he found himself at Barry Train Station.

Right back where it all began.

Vincent sat down on a bench. It was rush hour and busy people were hurrying home to flop down on couches and kick off their shoes. Vincent saw his old spot next to the snack machine. It was empty. He remembered his first day shining shoes and how happy he had been. How all he'd wanted was enough money to buy a bag of salt-and-vinegar chips and a sports drink that would hopefully turn his pee bluer than the Barry Public Pool. He remembered the big fat man, his first satisfied customer. And that wonderful tingly feeling. Vincent had almost forgotten how much he loved shoes. So much had happened. He felt like he'd been around the world and back again then around the world again. His grandfather was right. The shoe-cleaning kit was magic. But right now Vincent didn't feel so lucky. How had the best thing that ever happened to him turned into the worst?

As the last stragglers squeezed through the barriers, Vincent got up and headed home. The first thing he did was hug his mum and apologise for kicking Thom because it was the right thing to do. Vincent loved Thom, but sometimes he hated him too. Then he went to his room and pulled out his shoe-cleaning kit from under his bed. He checked all his brushes and polishes then packed them neatly back in the box. Vincent decided tomorrow he would return to the train station and set up his business again. At the very least it would take his mind off things.

As the weeks went by, Vincent became well known at Barry Train Station. Word spread across town that he could match any shoe colour exactly. Ladies queued to buy his special inserts for their favourite high heels. And the workers from FishyKittys came in droves to purchase his special spray that stopped their boots smelling like rotten fish. Some of their spouses came to buy it too. They said they secretly sprayed their husbands and wives when they came home from the factory and it worked a treat! The *Barry Daily* newspaper even sent a reporter to write a story about him. It was a full-page spread with a photo of Vincent sitting on his stool next to the snack machine, spraying a factory worker's boots. The headline said if there was a decline in Barry's divorce rate, it was probably because of Vincent's Fruity Boot Deodoriser.

Then one day, when Vincent was busy repairing a pair of cowboy boots, a lady appeared.

'Vincent! Is that you? What a wonderful surprise!'

Vincent recognised her face but couldn't for the life of him remember who she was. These days everyone in Barry seemed to know Vincent – especially since he'd had his picture in the paper.

'It's me, April's mum, from The Grandest Hotel on Earth.'

'Oh of course!' Vincent stood up. 'Now I remember. How's April?'

'She's doing great. I'm so glad I bumped into you. I've been wanting to say thank you for those inserts. She hadn't walked without holding my hand for six months and now she's at school playing chasings. She has her confidence back.'

'That's the best news!' said Vincent.

'April's young, but she's already fought a lot of battles. And she has bigger ones ahead unfortunately.'

Vincent nodded. He felt terrible for little April. She was such a sweet girl. 'Please tell her I said hi.'

'I will! She'd kill me for saying, but I think she had a bit of a crush on you, Vincent. She still talks about you. I think she liked to imagine you as a sort of big brother. She would have loved one of those. Anyway, we have much to be thankful for. I better run or I'll miss my train. Thank you again, Vincent. Bye.' April's mother disappeared through the barriers into the crowd.

Vincent sat down on his grandfather's stool. He thought about how everyone has a story, even though you can't always see it. But if you listen closely, you can feel it. Then a feeling came over him. Like that moment on a freezing day when a big cloud blocking the sun moves and the light and warmth hits your skin. It felt like the whole sky opened up.

It's not the knowing that's important!

It's the being!

Thom doesn't need to know I'm his big brother.

I am his big brother whether he knows it or not.

Vincent pulled out his notepad and pen and began scribbling down ideas. And from then on, in between customers, Vincent started making a pair of boots for Thom – just like Florence's. He figured if Thom had music at his toe tips, that might make him happier and calmer. He decided on yellow for the leather – just like The Grand – and instead of Bach, Vincent decided to program Thom's boots to play Erik Satie's Gymnopédie 1. His favourite.

After weeks of cutting and stitching and clamping and gluing, Thom's boots were finally ready. Vincent couldn't wait to give them to him. He packed up early and hurried home from the train station. When he arrived, Thom was standing at the kitchen table, trying to peel an egg.

'Hi Thom,' he said. There was a note of excitement in his voice for the first time since he'd left The Grand. 'I've got something for you!'

Thom didn't look up. He kept on peeling his egg.

Undeterred, Vincent held up the brand-new yellow boots. 'Boots, Thom.' Vincent pointed. 'For your feet.'

Thom looked at him blankly.

'Here. Let me help you.' While he continued to pick the shell from his egg, Vincent took off Thom's shoes, pulled the boots onto his feet and zipped them up. Vincent was quietly thrilled with his work. He squeezed around the toes. They were a perfect fit.

'Come, Thom. Walk with me,' he said, taking him by the hand.

Thom shoved the whole egg in his mouth and let Vincent lead him around the table. And when he heard the music, his eyes lit up like the flashing lights around the edges. He screamed and jumped up and down, which is what he did when he was really excited. All the commotion brought Vincent's mum and dad running into the kitchen.

And then Thom did something he'd never done before.

He hugged Vincent.

Not a long hug. Just a fleeting hug. But it was a hug all the same.

No one could believe it.

Vincent's eyes prickled with tears. *I love you, Thom*. He couldn't remember feeling as happy as he did right at that moment. And it surely was one of the grandest feelings on earth.

'I think he likes them,' said Vincent's mum, putting her arm around him.

'I think he does too,' agreed Vincent.

In fact Thom loved his boots so much he refused to take them off. Not even to go to bed and not even to take a bath. Of course you can't go without a bath for too long so to stop his boots getting ruined, his mum had to cover them with shopping bags held on with rubber bands. And they worked out a special manoeuvre where Thom plonked himself in backwards like a scuba diver off the side of the boat, leaving his boots high and dry on the edge of the bath.

And while Vincent didn't think he deserved all the credit, once Thom had his musical boots, everything just improved. Light returned to his mum's and dad's eyes and they began to enjoy each day rather than just trying to get through it. Mostly it was because along with some of the money Vincent had made shining shoes, his mum and dad finally had enough to send Thom to see the specialist in town.

He explained what was wrong with Thom and how to help him. So every day Vincent's mother sat down and tried to teach Thom how to talk. As well as do all the simple but extremely complicated things most people do without being taught how to do them. Like understanding how people feel by reading their face. Or how to play nicely and take turns. All these things were hard for Thom and that's why he had terrible tantrums. He was frustrated and frightened. The world didn't make sense to him and that was really scary.

One evening, Vincent was lying on his bed. He reached under and pulled out an old shoebox filled with all his sticky-taped up postcards of The Grand. He flicked through them the way he always did. He thought about Zelda and Dr Maaboottee and Rupert.

And Florence.

Despite all their promises to see each other and stay friends, Florence had never called. Vincent told himself she was probably too busy. Running The Grand was a huge job. He'd seen it for himself. But he could hardly lay all the blame at her feet. While Florence hadn't called him, he hadn't called her either. In truth Vincent found the idea of returning to The Grand too painful. Although he desperately wanted to tell everyone his news from home and see how big baby Tommy had grown and hold Min, he couldn't. To have been a part of The Grand family and then *not* a part of it hurt like hell. He knew he'd go back one day, but not yet. He couldn't bear it. Along with his postcards, Vincent packed up all his feeling about Florence and The Grand and the terrible vision. Then he put them in the box and shoved them back under the bed.

Vincent's mum poked her head round the door. 'There's a letter for you,' she said in a singsongy voice, waving an envelope at him.

Vincent immediately noticed the small hand-drawn picture of the hotel in the bottom left-hand corner. It was the official stationery of The Grand. He scrambled to his feet and grabbed the envelope. He waited for his mother to leave and then slowly opened it.

Dear Vincent,

We thought you might like to see a picture of Tommy.

He's learning how to use his trunk. He can pick things up and put them in his mouth and scratch himself when he has an itch! Tommy is now well over 100 kilograms — around what

206

he should have been when he was born. Winnie is a wonderful
mother and she is taking fine care of him. We do hope you'll
visit soon. Zelda says her sandals really could use a polish and
if you don't come up to visit us, she'll be coming down to visit you!
It's been busy here at The Grand, as always over summer.

Love to you and your family, Vincent.

Zelda and Dr Maaboottee

Vincent looked at the picture of Tommy. He had big eyes and tufts of wiry black baby hair on his head. Vincent thought there couldn't possibly be anything cuter. He felt a surge of warm pride. To think he had played a part in bringing Tommy into the world! Just then Thom came into the room. He leant against Vincent's bed and looked at the picture.

Vincent pointed at the elephant. 'Look, elephant! Remember? An elephant called Tom, like you.'

Thom grabbed the picture. He looked at it hard. 'Tom,' he said.

Vincent sat up. *Was that a cough or did he just say Thom?*

Vincent poked Thom in the chest. 'Thom.' Then he pointed at the elephant. 'Tom. Like you.'

Thom poked himself in the chest. 'Thom,' he said. He pointed at the elephant and said it again. 'Tom.'

That was no cough!

'MUM! DAD! COME QUICKLY! THOM JUST SPOKE! HE SPOKE!'

Vincent's mum and dad burst into the room.

'Thom just said his name, watch.'

Vincent pointed at Thom. 'Thom'

Thom looked at Vincent. He poked himself in the chest. 'Thom,' he said.

Vincent's mum and dad gasped. 'Good boy!' cried Vincent's mum, clapping. 'That's right! You're Thom! Good boy!'

Thom said it again. He seemed to enjoy making the sound with his mouth and the applause that followed. Vincent's mum and dad wrapped their arms around him and gave him a huge hug. Their eyes wide with happiness. Thom squirmed out of their embrace and bounded off like a kangaroo singing, 'Thom, Thom, Thom, Thom.'

Then Vincent's mum and dad wrapped their arms around him and the three of them hugged and laughed.

Straightaway, Vincent recognised it.

It's the vision! It's the future! The future has arrived. It's here!

CHAPTER 19

THE FUTURE

When Vincent woke the next morning, his chest felt heavy, as if someone had piled a full set of encyclopedias on top of it. And he had that feeling. Like sitting in the front carriage of a roller-coaster being hauled up a near vertical slope. The mechanical click as the cable drags the carriages to the top. The wobble of the wind, the staring straight ahead into nothingness as the skinny track stops climbing and falls away below.

Vincent was still unpacking polishes at the train station when he saw Rupert coming towards him. His stomach dropped.

'Vincent!' he said, trying to sound upbeat, but

it was obvious something was very, *very* wrong. Rupert's enthusiastic walk was flat. His smiling moustache a frown.

'What it is? What's wrong? Is it Florence?'

Rupert nodded. 'I'm afraid so. She wants to see you.'

Vincent threw his polishes and brushes into the box, grabbed his stool and jumped into the waiting car.

Driving up the mountain, Rupert filled him in on what had been going on. Apparently, the day he left, Florence fell ill. At first Dr Nelson thought it was a bad case of the flu. And then, when she didn't get better, he thought it must be something more serious, like pneumonia. But still Florence didn't get better. She got worse. Dr Nelson ordered a battery of tests.

And that's when they found it.

A tumour.

A tumour? Vincent's brain ticked and crackled over the word like a Geiger counter hovering over a lump of radioactive uranium. He didn't need to know what it was to know it was bad. Really bad.

'Is she in pain?'

Rupert nodded. 'A little.'

For the rest of the drive, Vincent and Rupert sat in silence.

As they drove through the gates of the hotel, the magnificence of the place flooded Vincent's soul. He had forgotten how beautiful it was. His mind struggled to hold the two things at once. How could something so terrible happen here? How was it possible?

Rupert took him straight to The Grand's hospital. Before they entered, he warned Vincent. 'You need to prepare yourself. Florry's very sick. She might not look like you rrr-remember.'

Vincent nodded. He didn't care, he just wanted to see her.

Florence's room was dark. The only light was a small lamp on the bedside table and the flashing machines that stood guard.

Bip . . . bip . . . . bip.

Florence lay flat on the bed. Her closed eyes looked like bruised and sunken shadows. A tube ran under her nose, another bandaged to her stick-thin arm. Draped across her tiny body was a red African shawl covered in elephants. And curled up in the crook of her neck was Emerson. Rupert went over, but Vincent hung back. It was terrifying. Seeing her like that. She was barely recognisable. And so small.

Rupert bent down and whispered in her ear. 'Florry, it's me, Rrr-rupert.'

Florence stirred but her eyes remained shut. 'Any word from Mummy and Daddy?'

'Not yet, dear. But there's someone here to see you.'

Vincent could see the struggle, just to even lift her eyelids.

'Vincent,' she whispered.

He picked up her hand and squeezed it gently. It was hard to speak. Everything looked the same as the vision.

'You came.'

'Of course I came.'

'I'm sorry I didn't call,' said Florence, her breath short and shallow.

'It's me who's sorry,' he said, pressing her hand to his cheek. 'I should have come. I wanted to. Every day. But . . .'

'I know. But you're here now.'

'I'm so sorry, Florence. I made such a mess of things. I never should have left you alone.'

'Don't feel bad. I was the one who sent you away, remember?'

'I didn't leave you much choice. I mucked up everything, more than you know.'

To stop himself crying Vincent dug his finger-nails into the palm of his clenched fist. He needed to be strong for her. He looked away, locking his eyes on her bedside table. There was a vase of fresh yellow flowers, an uneaten tomato sandwich and a smoking incense stick that smelt like licorice.

'From Zelda,' she said. 'And the shawl. It's ancient African medicine. She calls it *muti*.'

'What about your parents? Are they back?' asked Vincent.

'No. They're caught in the middle of a civil war. In Asia somewhere. They can't get out. I'm sure they'll be here soon.'

Vincent squeezed Florence's hand. He felt so terrible for her.

'What about the hotel?'

'Rupert's doing as much as he can and everyone's pitching in. But he can't keep doing his job and mine much longer. I really need to get better.'

Florence drifted in and out of consciousness. Vincent felt a darkness closing in. He wished he'd found a way to do his job and protect Florence at the same time. He cursed himself for going into the Mirrors of the Future Room. If he hadn't, would all this still be happening? Somehow it felt like this was all his fault.

Vincent looked at Florence.

'I can do it,' he heard himself say. A trail of light followed his words as they travelled through the room like a falling star.

'What?' Florence opened her eyes.

'I can run the hotel. Till you're back on your feet.'

Florence turned her head slowly towards him.

'No, Vincent. I can't ask you to do that. I'm sure my parents will –'

'Rupert can help me,' persisted Vincent, 'and Zelda and Dr Maaboottee. I know I mucked up, but I've learnt from my mistakes. It'll be different this time, I promise.'

'I know, Vincent.' She squeezed his hand. 'You . . . are . . . the . . . best . . . friend . . . I've . . .' Florence's eyes drifted shut and she fell back into sleep.

Florence hadn't said yes or no, but Vincent didn't think she was in any condition to make such a decision. As far as he was concerned, Florence didn't have a choice and neither did he. He hadn't been able to change the future, but he could take care of her now.

'Don't worry, Florence,' whispered Vincent. 'You concentrate on getting better. I'll take care of everything.' Vincent kissed Florence on the hand and hurried out the door.

Rupert was waiting outside.

'Rrr-righto. First things first.' Rupert handed Vincent a pair of brand-new emerald boots, just like Florence's.

Vincent's mind did cartwheels.

'But how did you know I'd offer to run the hotel? I . . . I didn't even know myself.'

'Oh come, come, come, Vincent! I know a lot of things. My moustache is an antenna. It picks up signals from the past, the present and the future. You should know that by now surely.' Rupert twitched his rainbow moustache – which did indeed look like a pair of antennae. 'I'm not the concierge at The Grandest Hotel on Earth for nothing, my boy.'

Vincent took off his shoes and pulled on the emerald boots. They were a perfect fit. He walked around in a small circle so he could hear them play.

'Beethoven,' announced Rupert with that strange mix of joy and fear you only ever hear in times of terrible trouble. 'Just to rrr-remind you to do things your own way. Even now. In fact especially now. Okay what's next? Ah, yes . . .'

Rupert pulled Min out of his top pocket and handed her to Vincent.

'Min!' He held her up against his cheek and she covered him in doggy kisses.

'And thirdly. There's no way you'll be able to rrr-run the place and travel up and down to Barry. You and your family will need to move in. There's no choice, I'm afraid.'

So Zelda was right, thought Vincent. Good things can come from bad. He had dreamt of bringing his family to The Grand since the day he arrived. He just wished their good fortune had not blown in on such ill winds. As long as Florence was suffering, how could he share his family's joy?

'I'll send a truck down and some movers to help you pack.'

Vincent nodded.

From somewhere off in the distance came a loud whirring sound, like a squadron of propeller planes flying low overhead.

'What's that?' asked Vincent.

'It's the hummingbirds. Ever since Florence became sick they've been going off.'

Vincent didn't know why but the sound of a field of hummingbirds beating their wings a million miles an hour made him nervous.

He looked down at his beautiful boots.

Just like the vision.

Suddenly it was all very real. He was in charge. He was going to have to run The Grandest Hotel on Earth!

Vincent's confidence vanished. He felt a crushing weight on his shoulders as if someone had slowly lowered a bus onto them. What was he thinking? He didn't know how to run a normal, straightforward hotel, let alone a place like The Grand.

'I'm not sure I can do this, Rupert.'

'On the contrary, Vincent, you're the *only* person who can do this.'

'But I'm not a Wainwright-Cunningham. I'm just a shoeshine boy.'

Rupert laughed. 'You're not just a shoeshine boy, Vincent! You're a shoe-shifter! The finest shoe-shifter I've ever seen. It was plain as day the first time I laid my moustache on you at Barry Train Station.'

'A what?'

'A shoe-shifter!' repeated Rupert.

'What's a shoe-shifter?'

'A shoe-shifter has an uncanny gift for putting themselves in other people's shoes. You know what it feels like to be them. That's what you do, Vincent. And not just some people's shoes. Any person's shoes. That's why you understand the true meaning of grand. And you don't just understand with your head, you understand with your heart. There's a big difference. You know with your heart why sometimes *everyone deserves a bit of grand*. Why do you think you always go to so much trouble with the shoes? It might seem like a small thing, but you can't soothe anyone's soul if they've got sore feet!'

A shoe-shifter. Rupert's words hoisted the bus back up, till it hovered just above Vincent's shoulders. 'I hope you're right.'

'Of course I am. Now chop, chop, chop. We've lots to do.'

CHAPTER 20

MOVING IN

Perhaps it does not surprise you, modern reader, to find out there were no objections from Vincent's family about moving into The Grandest Hotel on Earth. And despite having heard Vincent's stories about the place, driving through the gates, his entire family, including Thom, had their tongues hanging out like bits of defrosted steak.

'Breathe, everyone. Blink, everyone. Swallow, everyone. And don't pee your pants!' instructed Vincent.

On his first day behind the front desk, Vincent surprised himself. He felt strangely calm and in control. It's funny sometimes how the small things in life can throw us right off track while the big things light it up like nightlights on a runway.

The first thing Vincent did was take two maintenance workers to the Mirrors of the Future Room and nail the door shut. Then he had the name removed and nine heavy locks installed around the outside. The only way anyone would ever get into that room again was if they stuck a stick of dynamite under the door and blew it off.

The second thing Vincent did was ask his father if he could take over his old job shining shoes. He told Vincent he was more than happy to take time off from FishyKittys. He said he didn't think he was going to miss shoving massive, heavy trays of rotting seafood in and out of a 400-degree oven all day long. Not one bit!

The third thing Vincent did was take Rose over to the Grand Theatre. The new director from New York gave her a job as a stage sweeper. He said some of the best actors in the world started out that way, watching performances from the wings. And he said he didn't need to see the hundreds of emotions Rose could express with just her eyebrows to know that someday she was going to be famous.

'I can't believe it,' cried Rose. 'I've been waiting my WHOLE LIFE for this moment! And now it's here.'

And when he presented Rose with a real cape made out of satin that shimmered like the world from space she literally had to breathe into a paper bag to stop herself hyperventilating. The director made her sit down with her head between her legs so she didn't faint.

'This is so unglamorous,' she wailed. To which the director responded she wasn't the first actress to have this reaction, which made Rose start hyperventilating so hard she appeared to be auditioning for a horror movie.

'Did you hear that? He called me an actress. THE DIRECTOR JUST CALLED ME AN ACTRESS!'

Luckily Rose had her mouth in a paper bag, otherwise the director may have heard the most vile swearing ever to have come out of the mouth of a seven-year-old girl. (For some reason my co-author thinks that's hilarious so he too is now swearing enthusiastically into a paper bag and laughing like a pork chop.)

And while Vincent's mum just planned to do what she always did – without the cooking and the cleaning and the shopping – and look after Thom, it turned out she didn't have to. As soon as Thom walked into the lobby he ran straight for the elevator. He pushed the button and watched the light flick from one number to the next. When the doors opened, he rushed inside and lay down on the floor under Zelda's grand piano.

'You must be Thom. I've been expecting you. Welcome to The Grandest Hotel on Earth!'

Thom lay beneath the piano with his eyes closed and listened to Zelda's glorious playing. He was so happy he looked as if he was floating on the music itself. By lunchtime, Thom had learnt how to count from one to sixteen. He then moved to the stool in the corner where he pressed the buttons for the guests. Even more surprisingly, he greeted and smiled at each and every one of them. Which left Vincent's mother idle for the first time since Vincent was born eleven years ago.

At first she just sat in the lobby, dogs at her feet, and marvelled at the mysterious ways of The Grandest Hotel on Earth. She watched selfish guests become generous, the cold-hearted become kind, the cranky become sweet and the sad have their spirits lifted. In no time at all, it became apparent to Vincent that his mother had a natural gift for selecting just the right room. Rupert, who had trained under Nana Wainwright-Cunningham, said he hadn't seen such a talent since Nana herself. In fact he wept as he watched her work. 'Oh yes,' he sobbed, 'that's *exactly* the rrr-room Nana would have chosen. Bravo, bravo!' Which left Rupert worry-free and able to conduct guest orientations and help Vincent whenever needed. Which was often. The Grand was, after all, a HUGE operation and Vincent had much to learn. Supplies, deliveries, room maintenance, animal care, staff, food, entertainment, the upkeep of the grounds. But most importantly, ensuring every guest who walked through the gates was treated to a bit of grand.

Once his family was settled Vincent threw himself into his work and the hotel hummed along to the strains of Beethoven's ninth. With Vincent at the helm, the place ran as harmoniously as an orchestra that had played together a lifetime. Of course there were hiccups but no guest *ever* left without a bit of grand. And at the end of the day that was all that mattered. At lunchtimes and after work, Vincent sat with Florence. He brought her tomato sandwiches – which occasionally she nibbled – and read her letters from her parents, who were still stuck in a war zone. He told her stories about the guests and kept her up to date with the animals and all the day-to-day goings-on of the hotel. Every spare moment he had, Vincent was by her side. Sometimes he told himself he could see some colour back in her golf-ball cheeks or a bit more meat on her protruding bones. But it was wishful thinking more than anything.

Then one lunchtime when Vincent arrived, Florence was sitting up. She ate a whole tomato sandwich and two whatever-flavour-you-think-of balls.

'What flavour?' asked Vincent.

'Pancakes and maple syrup,' she said. 'You?'

'Cheese and bacon again! Would you believe it? As soon as I pop one in my mouth I can't think of anything else!' Which made Florence smile. Her funny Vincent.

'I've never had a friend like you,' she said, licking her fingers. 'No one's ever taken care of me. We Wainwright-Cunninghams are *not* taken care of. It's not what we do.'

'Well, maybe we met each other at exactly the right time,' said Vincent. 'You needed help and I needed to help. We sort of saved each other.'

'You have saved me, Vincent. You have. I don't know how I can ever repay you.'

'You don't need to, Florence. We're friends remember. That's what friends do.'

That night, Vincent slept the sleep of the gods. He woke next morning fresh as the mountain air itself, full of sunshine and hope. But by day's end, Florence had taken a turn for the worse. When Vincent arrived at the hospital, something felt different. Her pocket dog, Emerson, was curled up right on top of her heart. Florence didn't open her eyes or lift her index finger the way she usually did to signal she knew Vincent was in the room. He could tell she didn't have the energy to even listen. So he just sat down by her side and held her hand.

Florence looked so small. Her emerald glasses enormous on her now-hollow cheeks. Her cinnamon hair dull and brittle. Vincent's mind flew up the mountain to the platform where they ate tomato sandwiches and watched the birds soar. He tried to picture the old healthy Florence, the one who flew up the front steps two at a time or thrashed him in a rocking-horse race. But he couldn't. It felt like she was slipping away.

A lightning bolt flashed in the distance, lighting up the whole room.

A storm was coming.

'Looks like we're in for a rough night, Florry,' he whispered to her. 'I'm just going to baton down the hatches and check on the guests. I'll be back as soon as I can, promise.'

Vincent pulled the red African shawl covered in elephants up around Florence's shoulders. He lit a couple of Zelda's *muti* incense sticks that smelt like licorice then hurried off to the hotel. As he ran across the grounds, the weather grew wilder and wilder. Bolts of lightning lit up the Mabombo Ranges as if it was daylight. The hummingbirds, confused, began beating their wings, filling the valley with a roar like a million motorcycles. And as he scrambled up the front steps, hailstones the size of golf balls began pelting down from the sky.

Guests had gathered in the lobby to watch the storm. Even those staying in the Extreme Weather Room. Vincent saw his family. Thom gently clutching his pocket dog, Rhubarb, Rose in her shimmering cape. His mum and dad, arm in arm, their whole bodies remoulded by happiness. Each and every one of their lives transformed by The Grandest Hotel on Earth.

Once Vincent was sure everything and everyone was all right, he grabbed a raincoat and headed for the door.

'Vincent! You can't go out in that!' yelled Rupert. 'A Mabombo storm is not to be messed with, trust me.'

'I have to,' cried Vincent. 'She's alone. I can't leave her alone. Not tonight.' Tears fell down Vincent's cheeks. He felt as if, one by one, the lights on his runway were going out.

Rupert nodded. 'Here. Give Min to me. I'll take care of things back here. Take the side path. It's longer but safer. And stay away from the trees.'

'Thank you, Rupert.'

'Come here,' he said, tucking Min into his top pocket. He squeezed Vincent in a bear hug. 'Kiss Florry for me.'

Vincent flew down the front steps, hail exploding all around him like ice bombs. He remembered Rupert's advice and took the path that ran along the side of the hotel. The dark peaks of the Mabombo Ranges and his flashing boots helped him navigate as he ran as fast as he could towards the hospital.

Then something strange happened. Vincent heard noises. It sounded like a voice. And it was singing. *Surely no one's out in this?* There it was again. Like a spirit released from the Mabombo's mighty black peaks. But it wasn't coming from the mountains. It was coming from the ground. Without slowing Vincent looked down. *My boots! It's coming from my boots.*

His boots had never sung before.

It was as if they had tuned into some radio station far out in the universe or a fireside song from an ancient civilisation way back in time. Lashed by the hail and rain, Vincent kept running. The voice swirled up around his body, then tumbled into his chest, wrapping itself around his heart like a warm blanket. Strings came in. Then stamping, mountain-ous horns. And above the horns that voice. Calling from the mountaintops and the deserts and the ancient deep blue seas.

Vincent's legs gave way and he fell to the ground. 'Argh!'

He lay on the sodden earth. Part of him wished he could sink beneath it and part of him didn't. He kicked his boots into the ground and cried.

Not Florence. Please. Not Florence. Please not Florence.

A flash of lightning lit up the valley.

Vincent saw something next to his arm. It was the emerald polish he'd used to clean Florence's boots.

Another flash of lightning. Vincent realised he was in the Junkyard of Broken and Abandoned Dreams. Right next to the shrine he'd made to leave behind his dream to save Florence from the terrible thing in her future. The terrible thing that had now arrived.

Vincent picked up the polish. Struggling to see in the rain and darkness, he placed it back on the top of his shrine. Then Vincent spoke into the night. It seemed crazy, but he didn't care: 'This is my dream for Florence, the grandest girl on earth. I dream that she always has a bit of grand, wherever she may be.'

CHAPTER 21

FAMILY BUSINESS

The light of dawn woke him. At first Vincent had no idea where he was. And then he saw Emerson rising and falling, fast asleep on Florence's chest. Relief flooded his soul. She was alive. Florence was still alive. So alive she was even snoring a little. Vincent smiled as he listened to her short sharp snorts. There was something reassuring about them. Something so alive. Without waking her, he tiptoed out of the room and headed back to the hotel.

Outside the skies had begun to clear. The hummingbirds had ceased beating their wings and a wet, golden silence filled the valley. As he walked into the lobby, the smell of coffee and croissants and melting chocolate wafted in from the Breakfast Hall.

Vincent's family was still at the window, watching the last storm clouds disappear over the mountains.

'Bow!' said Thom, pointing at a rainbow stretching from one side of the valley to the other.

'That's right, Thom! A rainbow,' said Vincent.

Thom turned and smiled. 'Wainbow.'

Vincent's dad looked him up and down. 'What happened to you?'

Vincent looked at his uniform. It was covered in mud. 'It's a long story.'

'You'll have to fill us in over breakfast.'

'I will.'

Vincent's mum gave him a kiss. She took Thom's hand. 'Let's go see the giraffes, shall we?' And they wandered off to the breakfast room.

'Bags not sit next to Vincent,' said Rose, tap-dancing after them. 'He smells like elephant poop.'

Vincent sniffed his jacket. Rose was right. He did pong a bit.

Before joining his family for breakfast, Vincent showered and changed his uniform. Then he headed out onto the balcony to check the grounds for storm damage. A tree on Fin's Island had fallen, but otherwise it looked like everything had survived the night. The lake, a mirror, joined the ends of the rainbow together, capturing the reflection of the hotel in a colour-rimmed bubble of light. Inside the bubble, a perfect world, so perfect it looked as if it might float away.

Vincent saw a guest riding a llama around the lake towards the hotel. He pulled out his binoculars to make sure there was a pooper-scooper nearby and couldn't quite believe his eyes.

It wasn't a guest.

It was Florence! She was up! And dressed in her milk-blue velvet skirt and beaded and feathered hand-stitched jacket, her cinnamon hair glinting in the sun.

Vincent ran down the stairs three at a time. 'Florence! Florence!'

He ran around the lake.

'Florence!' Vincent reached up to help her off her llama. He wrapped his arms around her and squeezed her as gently as he could although every atom of his being wanted to squeeze her as tight as a pair of five-sizes-too-small pants. 'Oh, Florence.

You're all right! Are you all right? You're all right! Shouldn't you be in bed?'

'Dr Nelson checked me out this morning. He said I've made a remarkable recovery. Nothing short of a miracle! In fact those were his exact words. He said he still wants to run a few tests and keep up my treatment, but it looks like I might be on the mend,' she said, smiling.

'That's the best news ever. Ever, ever, ever!'

'You sound like Rupert.'

'You're right. I do!'

They both laughed.

'What about that storm last night?' said Florence, her cheeks rosy and aglow. 'Wasn't it grand? Let's have breakfast – I'm starving!'

Florence looked around the Breakfast Hall full of contented guests eating and laughing. At the windows giraffes chewed carrots like gumballs while the band played the kind of happy jazz that had at least one guest at each table up and dancing.

'Oh, Vincent! Look at what a magnificent job you've done.'

This time it was Florence's turn to cry. She hugged Vincent tight.

'I'm so glad you're happy, Florence, but more than anything I'm just so glad you're all right.'

'Well, after tomato toast and a stack of pancakes I will be!'

Vincent couldn't help fussing as he sat Florence down at a table with his mum and dad and Rose and Thom. Before long they were joined by Luz and Tracee and Rupert and Zelda and Dr Maaboottee. So happy to see Florence back on her feet Luz and Tracee did the 'living my best life' dance around the table. Rupert broke down in a flood of tears and engulfed Florence in a bear hug. 'Florry, my Florry. We've got our Florry back!' Unable to wait for Rupert to release her, Zelda and Dr Maaboottee joined in and wrapped their arms around the two of them.

After the storm and Florence's miraculous recovery, everyone was ravenous.

'I see you like eggs, Thom,' said Zelda, as she tucked into a spicy chip omelette with a side order of Swahili doughnuts.

Thom looked at his plate piled high with fried eggs, poached eggs, scrambled eggs and eggs every-other-which-way eggs can be cooked.

'Eggs. Yano,' said Thom. He slid off his chair and tugged Vincent's arm.

'What do you want, Thom?'

'Yano. For Vincence.' Then he ran towards the band, who were taking a break, and crawled up onto the piano stool. He put his hands on the keys and began playing Erik Satie's Gymnopédie No.1.

Perfectly.

The entire room fell silent.

And still.

Everyone was astonished. Even the giraffes stopped chewing and turned their heads to watch as Thom's small fingers danced gracefully and tenderly across the keys.

Vincent felt so proud to be his big brother. And as he looked across at his parents' faces, at one particular moment Vincent could have sworn he saw their hopes and dreams return, floating in through the Breakfast Hall windows like a great big yellow hot air balloon.

'I think we just found our new pianist for the lobby,' announced Rupert.

Vincent and Florence nodded. Under the table, Florence grabbed Vincent's hand and squeezed it tight.

In the months that followed, Florence finished her treatment and was given the all clear from

Dr Nelson. Every day she became stronger and stronger. And together Vincent and Florence ran The Grandest Hotel on Earth.

One morning, somewhere in between inspecting goggles and tanks for the Aquatic Room and checking the atmospheric pressure in the Cloud Room, Vincent knew the time had come. 'You know, Florence, you're well enough now to run The Grand on your own. You don't need us anymore.'

Florence stopped what she was doing. She pushed her green glasses back up her nose and looked at Vincent. It was a moment before she spoke.

'Yes. You're right of course. I can. But if I'm honest – I hope my ancestors aren't listening – it's pretty hard and lonely running this place all by myself. And realistically I don't think my parents will be back any time soon. There's always another mountain mist frog in need of saving. Being sick made me realise something, Vincent. Something I'd never thought about. Letting other people help you is just as grand as helping them. If not grander. Which is why I've been wanting to ask you something.'

'Ask away.'

'Do you think you and your family might

consider staying? We have a school. All the workers' children attend, myself included when I have the time.' Florence bit her top lip and scrunched up her nose.

Vincent didn't say anything for what seemed to Florence like the longest time.

He swallowed and then finally he spoke.

'Well, if *I'm* honest, Florence, while I've loved running The Grand, there's nothing I love more than shining people's shoes. I've even been teaching Thom how to mix polishes; he's a natural. Although I think he prefers piano. And Dad and I want to go into business together. Mr D'Silva's already offered to put up the money. You wouldn't believe how many orders we get a week for my Happy Feet High-Heel Inserts and my Fruity Boot Deodoriser. Dad and I thought we'd call it Barry Boots 'n' Shoes.'

Florence, who without realising it had been holding her breath, exhaled. 'That's perfect. We need someone to shine the guests' shoes and you need customers and a place to run your family business!'

It occurred to Vincent that now his shoeshine business really *was* a family business!

Vincent's mind sparked with possibility. 'I know my mother would love to keep helping with room selection. And Thom and Rose would be happy if they never had to leave.'

'That's settled then,' said Rupert, who appeared from out of nowhere, carrying something large under his arm. 'What do you think?'

Rupert plugged the thing into the wall and held it up. It was a brand-new neon sign: 'Barry Boots 'n' Shoes at The Grand'.

Vincent knew better than to ask how he knew.

'Come, come, come, we have so much to do!' declared Rupert. Arm in arm, the three of them headed back to the lobby, Rupert in the middle, his enthusiastic hips bumping into theirs with each and every step.

And so it was, Vincent and his family moved in permanently to The Grandest Hotel on Earth. Florence's family completed their Gene Bank for the world's endangered species and fast moved on to the next grand project. As was their destiny. Another five Wainwright-Cunninghams even made their way into the *Guinness World Records* in the same time it took me and my co-author to write this book!

And Vincent went back to shining shoes with his grandfather's shoe-cleaning kit in the red leather chair next to the elevator. To this day, Florence and

Vincent still race around the rocking-horse racetrack and take lunch on the Platform for the Reckless, eating tomato sandwiches, pocket dogs in their laps, eyes to their binoculars, watching wheeling eagles fly. All the while serenaded by their Beethoven-and-Bach-playing emerald boots.

To think!

All that.

From one little MOMENTOUS moment.

A NOTE ABOUT MY GRAND CO-AUTHOR, FINLEY WRIGHT CURNOW

In 2017, my very favourite godson, nine-year-old Finley Wright Curnow became very sick. He was diagnosed with an incurable brain tumour. Living just across the railway line, I visited Finley often. But as he became more unwell, sometimes I would write to him and leave letters on his front verandah. One day I told him about my idea for this book and asked Finley if he could help me create The Grandest Hotel on Earth. Perhaps he had some ideas for rooms? No mind if he didn't. I knew just being sick took up a lot of energy.

Well, the very next day, I received a letter from Finley.

Did he have ideas for rooms?

Did he what!

He had *incredible* ideas for rooms!

The Levitation Room, the Roller-coaster Room, the Baby Memories Room . . . these were all Finley's ideas.

But there was more. And one of his ideas struck me like a bat. 'A Room of Mirrors of the Future. The shoeshine boy discovers the secret room and sees the bad future of the grandest girl and has to alter time to save her.'

BOOM!

It was like an explosion in my head.

Just like the one Vincent experienced when he entered the Mirrors of the Future Room.

Writing this now I am reminded how much I am indebted to Finley for this story. How much it is his story too. And I'm reminded what a terrible loss it is that Finley is no longer around to tell us all his wonderful, incredible, brilliant ideas. He had his own dreams and I know he would have grown into the grandest man.

Unfortunately, he didn't get that chance, but together *we* have the chance to try to stop what happened to Finley from happening to other beautiful kids. Which is why a portion of the author's proceeds from the sale of this book will go to the Children's Cancer Fund. You too can donate at: donate.ccia.org.au/donations.

If together we can help find a cure, would that not be THE GRANDEST thing ever? Even grander than a baby elephant!

ABOUT THE AUTHOR

LISA NICOL is a writer and documentary-maker. Her feature documentary *Wide Open Sky*, about a children's choir in outback NSW, won the Audience Award for Best Documentary at the 2015 Sydney Film Festival.

Her first children's book *The Ballad of Dexi Lee* was illustrated by artist Lucy Culliton. Her second children's book *Dr Boogaloo and the Girl Who Lost Her Laughter* is currently being adapted as a musical for the stage.

Lisa lives on the east coast of Australia with her three children and a dog who totally stinks.

ACKNOWLEDGEMENTS

Vincent and the Grandest Hotel on Earth is the most special book to me.

It will forever be the only book I got to write with Finley and that, as Rose and Finley would say, 'sucks'. So my biggest thanks goes to Finley Wright Curnow, my co-author, for his beautiful, original and magical ideas.

In case anyone was wondering, all dogs lounging in front of lobby fires are chocolate Labradors who only eat chocolate dog food. And every one of them is called Maple. Maple 1, Maple 2, Maple 3 – you get the idea.

And since a trip to The Grand is unfortunately not something everyone will be chosen for, as a hidden extra I have been permitted to reveal some of the 'Find Your Inner Sloth' class teachings:

Sloth teaching #1: Always get room service instead of coming down for meals – just press the room-service button.

Sloth teaching #2: Always drop by at friends' houses around mealtimes so you never have to cook.

Sloth teaching #3: Where possible, go nude – saves you having to wash your clothes.

Perhaps the other big contributor I have to thank is my publisher, Holly Toohey. Holly has been a solid supporter of *The Grand* since before a word was written. And when I did hand her those first words it's fair to say I was dizzy and delusional after too long going round and round at Tenzing, the Grand's rotating restaurant. But instead of mourning in the Junkyard of Broken and Abandoned Dreams, Holly handed me a detailed map, sent me to the You Can Do Way Better Than That Room, and a few months later I walked out with a publishable book. Also at Penguin Random House, I'd like to thank Laura Harris for green lights and Tim Tams and my patient editor, Jess Owen, for putting up with such second-book stroppiness!!! (And so many exclamation marks.)

Credits are also due to the imaginative Rohan Smith, who sent me a million cracking ideas for rooms, including the Time of Day Room, where it's whatever time of day you want it to be (that unfortunately didn't feature in the story but is in fact on the 7th floor, turn left after the elevator). He is also responsible for the never-melting chocolate couch in the Edible Room. At the same time I met Rohan, I met Hayley and Grace, one of whom had the brilliant idea for the rocking-horse racetrack. I just wish I could remember who! Apologies and thanks to both of you!

Special thanks to Katy Pike for early readings of the manuscript and her illuminating explanations of what the story is actually about (thank goodness someone knew). Anna Craney for listening to my struggles, untangling the meaningless from the meaningful and ambient guidance on all things story. Patrick Mangan for all things persnickety, which is never to be sniped at. (Yes, I know that's two 'all things' in close proximity, Patrick. Now three.) My writers' group for their top-shelf editorial advice and support: Marion, Denise, Jenny, Wendy, Debra, Sarah, Tracey, Katrina, Maala and Amanda.

My agent, Sara Crowe, and everyone at Pippin Properties. So thrilled to be a Pip.

And lastly to my own children: Atticus, Franny and Levon (inventor of the Infinity Room) for being the grandest co-dreamers a dreamer could wish for.